COCKATOO

Yashraj Goswami is a writer, poet and teacher based in Delhi. His words have appeared in various publications, including *Indian Express*, *Huffington Post India*, *Scroll.in* and *DNA*. His poems and short stories have been widely anthologized. His writing gently probes the varied shades and expressions of masculinity in modern India. *Cockatoo* is his first book.

COCKATOO

YASHRAJ GOSWAMI

PAN

First published in 2023 by Pan
an imprint of Pan Macmillan Publishing India Private Limited
707 Kailash Building
26 K. G. Marg, Delhi 110001
www.panmacmillan.co.in

Pan Macmillan, The Smithson, 6 Briset Street, London EC1M 5NR
Associated companies throughout the world
www.panmacmillan.com

ISBN 978-93-89109-95-5

1 3 5 7 9 8 6 4 2

Typeset in Crimson Roman by SŪRYA, New Delhi
Printed in India by Gopsons Papers Pvt. Ltd., Noida.

Contents

Prologue

THE WINTER IN Hyderabad is pleasant, a welcome change from the brisk winds of northern India. And a respite from the sticky, stifling heat of the south. The city's air carries the delicate strains of the azan and the rich aroma of spices.

But the air inside the flat is rank – it smells like him. For the past four days, no one has entered or left the house. Two rolled newspapers are stuck in the narrow handle of the grille door. Two more lie untouched, uncared for on the doorstep. The envelopes are a little luckier. Thanks to the kindness of the neighbours, who pushed them in from the narrow space between the door and the floor, they have found their way inside. They too lie unopened, unseen – but on the opposite side of the grille door. They too suffer, but not without dignity.

The weather is cool, yet his body is slick with sweat. Everything in the house that could be eaten has been consumed. Hunger has begun to play mind games with him. But he would still prefer starvation to facing another human being. He goes to the kitchen, thinking there must be some leftover cola in the fridge. From the first gulp, he can tell that the cola has lost its fizz. It's just a bittersweet liquid now. But there's enough sugar in it to keep him going for the next few hours. And after that? Must there always be an after?

The sound of the doorbell pierces through the stale air of the flat, like the shriek of a bird ambushed by a stray tomcat. He stands frozen in the kitchen. His heart begins to sink. There are feathers and blood streaks all over him. He waits, motionless, hoping the visitor goes away. Suddenly he wishes to shrink himself, to shed his broad frame and long limbs. He is afraid his stature will expose him. They will realize he is inside. However, with his adult body, he can confront the cat this time. He can even rescue the bird. If he can't save the bird, at least he can kill the cat and exact revenge. He is capable of more than wailing on his own.

The bell goes off again. This time, it's being pressed harder, perhaps even with exasperation. His stomach is churning. His knees fold as he can no longer support himself. He is now crouching. There are more feathers and more blood. The wild shrieks, feathers and bloody streaks are choking him.

After that, there is silence. Have they left?

With long strides, he walks out of the kitchen towards his bedroom. If only the world could be enveloped in silence. He wouldn't mind stepping out if the constant clamour of demands, desires and deeds could be muffled. It seemed like a simple wish. But it would not be granted. Letters would still be pushed through the door; emails would be sent informing him that he has lost his job, and the phone would still ring to confirm the news ('Is it true what we heard about the company you work for? Is it really going to shut down?').

He gradually sinks onto the bed by degrees, as if suspended by invisible threads. Then, raising his head, he reaches for his journal with his long arm. He scribbles laboriously. Sometimes the hand refuses to obey, limp from exhaustion, but then recalling that he has just guzzled cola, his hand ploughs on.

It becomes increasingly challenging. He pushes the journal aside and rises, overcome by his own odour. His eyes are moist. 'What happened, baby?' His mother's soothing voice asks. 'Why are you so upset? Does your tummy hurt?' He wishes to return to her. Also, say goodbye in person. But saying goodbye is the most difficult.

As he slides the window open, the house sighs with relief. It finally breathes after what seems like an eternity. The winters in Hyderabad are indeed pleasant. He leans against the window. Some children are playing in the compound below. He observes them for a few moments. When one of them looks up by accident, he staggers back a couple of steps, as if caught in illegal activity. Why should he be scared of these mice? Suddenly, he is awash with sympathy. They would have to give up their game. They'd disperse and hide in their holes for days. But why should he care about them or anyone else? Nobody thinks of him before they leave. He is on the seventh floor. How high is he above the ground? How many feet above sea level?

He emerges from the window head first, then limb by limb, like a creature breaking free from its cocoon. The children below are amused at first, then excited. Is he a superhero?

He sits on the window ledge, his legs dangling outside. The bird shrieks again. Louder this time. Feathers and blood. Blood and feathers. His heart begins to thump, but he steadies himself. He, too, has to go. He, too, will have to fly.

The Invitation

Neera cursed herself for attending the wedding reception. She should have turned down the invitation and followed her instincts. It was 11 p.m., and the roads were deserted. Every now and then, a car or bike zipped past her, penetrating the silence. The driver of the previous cab she had booked had cancelled, and the next had not arrived in over ten minutes. Worse, it appeared that it was about to rain. Her lips pursed.

Please wait ... connecting you to your nearest cab.

The message flashed with that irritating, never-ending timer. For a moment, Neera considered going back and asking the hostess for assistance. Maybe Paromita could get her a car. But she was too preoccupied with seeing off other guests and attending to those who remained. Wasn't taking an autorickshaw preferable to asking Paromita for a favour? However, there was no sign of an autorickshaw either. She decided to try her luck one final time, tapping the 'find cab' button on the app. A shared cab was only seven minutes away. It wasn't the best time to be picky, she reasoned, before clicking 'confirm pickup'.

Neera had expected to find other passengers in the car when she climbed inside, but there were none. Regardless, she chose to sit in the front seat. There was always the possibility that others could be picked up along the way, and she didn't want to be stuck between strangers.

'Hello, madam,' said the young driver.

'Hello, *aur pickups hain kya?*'

'No more pickups, madam. There was one, but he cancelled, so it's just you for the time being.'

'Nice ... do you speak English? I mean, your English is nice,' she added, wondering if that sounded patronizing. To redeem herself, she laughed nervously.

'Madam, where will the drop be?'

'Hauz Khas,' she said.

The driver turned on the car's overhead light. Neera could now see a young boy with big, bright eyes. He bent and began to fumble for something.

'Anything wrong?'

'It's only my phone, madam ... Here it is!' He smiled, holding up a tiny phone. Then he turned off the light.

'Hauz Khas, right?' enquired the driver, his gaze drawn to the other cell phone, which was docked in a slot next to the steering wheel. He traced the entire route highlighted in blue on the map with his index finger.

'Do you know how to get there?'

Neera raised her head after fastening her seat belt. 'Actually, I don't visit this area very often. I am just as inexperienced as you. Or perhaps even more than you!'

She looked at the driver again, this time more intently. The pale-yellow light from the street lamps filtered through the windshield, flirting with his face and leaving it partially illuminated.

'So—?' He cocked his brow.

Neera leaned forward, her face dangerously close to his, to look at the screen. A strange sensation gripped her. Was the air getting colder?

'Yes, this appears to be fine,' she muttered, hastily withdrawing to fiddle with the seatbelt once more.

'May I help you?' he asked as he changed gears and pressed the accelerator.

'Oh, no ... it's just ... it's done. The belt was a bit loose,' Neera explained. She drew her delicately embroidered shawl closer to her. 'Could you turn off the AC?'

'Sure,' he replied. 'Isn't this rain very sudden?'

Thank goodness she was carrying the shawl, which was only meant to be an accessory. This December had started out relatively warm and, as the boy mentioned, the rain had been unexpected. There had been no indication of its arrival until about half an hour ago, and now it was drizzling. She turned her attention to the app screen again, where it said, 'You're on your way' above the driver's name, Chandar.

She wouldn't have gone to the wedding if it hadn't been for Paromita's insistence. 'Please, Neera, come – for the sake of old times. If Kishor had been alive, he would have definitely come. After all, we were neighbours for twenty years,' she'd said over the phone. Even though Kishor had only been dead for four years, it seemed like a different era to Neera. Surprisingly, she had handled Kishor's loss well.

She had moved into a larger flat and a better neighbourhood, leaving behind Paromita, who, she suspected, secretly envied her. Neera had no children of her own, and with Koel – Kishor's daughter from his first marriage – in California, there was hardly anyone to whom Neera could present the bereaved, widowed version of herself. Not that she had sobbed hysterically at his death; she was far too poised for it. She had, however, shed some solemn tears. Even in her grief, Neera never lost her grace. She'd lost the only pair of eyes that would have been wet when hers would shut forever. Was it his death that she mourned? Or that no one would be left to mourn hers? She knew it was a waste of time to think about it. But these thoughts ambushed her. Then, in order to keep them away, a distraction – a bigger waste of time – had to be found.

'So, Chandar, how long have you been driving this cab?'

'A long time, madam. I used to work in Mumbai before. The work hours are bad here. I can get up to twelve rides a day, some of them very early in the morning. Especially for the airport. But I've decided to give it everything I've got.'

Neera had not expected such a genuine response. Was it his perky smile that made his face stand out? She felt like indulging him.

'Do you enjoy driving?' she asked, looking out of the window. Outside, it continued to drizzle.

'Yes, madam. You know, I want to prove myself. I can't afford to be a lost child. I used to play a lot of cricket, go to the gym and hang out with my friends. But it's all about work now.'

'Do you no longer play or exercise?'

'No, who has the time?' he responded, as if surprised by the question.

She secretly examined his chest. He appeared in good shape.

'Arey, madamji, this is nothing,' he said. His left hand flew from the steering wheel and landed on the dashboard, searching for his other phone. 'Would you like to see what I used to look like when I worked out?'

Neera felt exposed and embarrassed. She had thought her actions were subtle. He opened the phone's image gallery without waiting for her approval. Neera couldn't decide whether to be annoyed or amused by his antics. She couldn't bring herself to say what she was thinking or what she ought to have said: *Thanks, but no thanks.*

This boy was tactless, like Paromita. Neera had never been particularly fond of her old neighbour. She missed the cool indifference of her Parsi neighbours when she was a girl growing up in Mumbai. Her family used to take pride in being one of the only four non-Parsi families living in an all-Parsi colony in Lower Parel.

Not only was Paromita tactless, but she was also intrusive. They fought frequently when she lived next door. Of course, Neera couldn't compete with her neighbour's decibel levels. She began sputtering Marathi swear words whenever she was losing the battle. Eventually, Kishor had to step in every time. That was the thing about Kishor: No one could stay angry in his company. He could diffuse the situation with a single joke.

After all was said and done, she couldn't forget how Paromita and her family had helped her in the aftermath of Kishor's death.

It would have been unkind of Neera to have declined the invitation. And then there was Aditi, Paromita's cheerful daughter, who used to come to Neera with her maths problems. What a fine-looking woman she had grown into. At such a young age, she was the regional manager of a reputable private bank. Neera would not have gone to the wedding reception if it hadn't been for Aditi and the fear of being labelled ungrateful. She could have used Koel's late-night flight to dodge the invitation. But she liked Aditi; she had watched her grow up. She had decided to give Aditi her favourite perfume as a present. Neera's own daughter, if she had had one, would have been Aditi's age.

Neera had told herself many times she wasn't cut out to be a mother. Kishor would always remind her of the conversation they'd had about this topic on their second date. One of the first things she had asked him was whether he read books. Kishore had joked that he liked books from a distance. 'I mean, I am not opposed to books so long as I don't have to read them. You can bring all your books to my home – nay – our home, if that's what you mean,' he had replied, making Neera blush.

As their date was coming to an end, Kishor had asked Neera if she liked children. She paused before responding. The Arabian Sea in front looked hungry enough to swallow the last rays of sunlight edging the horizon. It was nearly dark. Neera, in her mid-thirties at the time, stood silently on Marine Drive, the sea breeze ruffling up her hair.

'Neera ...?'

'I like them, Kishor, but from a distance. I mean, I don't mind them as long as I don't have to raise them myself,' she explained, unsure whether he would find her joke funny. To her surprise, Kishor laughed in his usual, uninhibited manner, which Neera always found a little embarrassing in public. 'I've already got one of my own. Just don't get rid of her!' he exclaimed, squeezing her shoulder.

As a result, it was decided they would not have children together. But why did he still bring up that anecdote? At a party, a family gathering (his family), and on a regular basis at their monthly fine-dining nights. He always laughed deeply, just like he had on their date. Had he actually found it amusing? Every single time?

Chandar handed over the phone to Neera. On the screen was a topless image of a man who appeared barrel-chested and glazed in sweat. Neera's head was buzzing from the wine she had consumed at the wedding. Though she thought the gesture would be completely inappropriate, she felt compelled to touch his biceps to see if they had shrunk from the size in the photograph. He swiped the screen before she could react – or act on her impulse.

'This, madam, is my girlfriend,' Chandar said casually.

'Oh! You have a girlfriend?' The moment she asked it, she realized how ridiculous her question sounded. A handsome twenty-something man with his own car – of course, he could have a girlfriend.

'I have three girlfriends, madam. But she's the one I'd like to marry. I love her. My *mausi* doesn't approve of her. So I have told her clearly: "I will marry Shabbo, no matter what you say." The others are just for fun. They constantly bother me with phone calls. I can't spend all day on the phone. But they don't get it and become fussy. They're trouble, these girls. I prefer women.'

'Mausi?'

'Yes, my aunt, I live with her. This is her car.'

'Your parents?'

'As good as dead,' Chandar said sharply.

'How peculiar! And I guess Shabbo is your ...'

'Yes, her name is Shabina, and she is my real girlfriend. She is a really nice girl. She taught me English.'

'Shabina,' Neera muttered to herself. 'Sounds like a Muslim name. Is that the issue?'

'No, no, it's not as simple. The thing is, Shabina isn't ...' Chandar grew solemn. The torrent of his words slowed for the first time on the ride. 'Madamji, the thing is Shabina is not like other people. My girlfriend is ...'

'It's fine; you don't need to tell me. I shouldn't have asked.' Neera's head was starting to feel heavy now. 'What fun is a love story without any drama, isn't it?' she said, running her fingers through her hair.

'Hmm ...'

Neera had also desired a dramatic marriage proposal. But expecting that from Kishor was ridiculous. He was far from dramatic. 'Who should I ask for your hand in marriage, now that both your parents are gone? Your landlady?' he had enquired earnestly, and for a moment, Neera had taken him seriously. Her relationship with Kishor went swimmingly. Uneventful, but smooth. She didn't have much to be upset about. She had even grown to love him after a while. Although Kishor did not offer the fiery passion she had craved in her youth, he did provide her with ease – much more comforting and durable. She only needed to move to the left side of the bed. For conversation or copulation. For compliments or criticism. Even if she wanted to find someone who could be blamed for all the insufficiencies of her life, she only had to look to Kishor as he snored his way through the night. They were perfectly matched in many ways, she had thought; she was desired by many but wanted by few, and he was wanted by many but desired by few. Wasn't it love that she felt at ease with him?

'Is the seat belt fine? Or is it still loose?' Chandar asked, turning to face her.

Neera gave a nod. His eyes lingered a moment too long on her cleavage. The shawl had slipped off her shoulder, and she looked in the rear-view mirror at her hazy reflection. She knew she looked pretty for a forty-eight-year-old woman, with her supple skin and reasonably firm breasts. She adjusted her shawl to prevent her breasts from accidentally revealing themselves.

The rain had stopped. Neera rolled down the window, letting the moist breeze in.

'Would you like to see photos of my other girlfriends, madam?' Chandar asked, as the car came to a halt at a crossing.

'No, thanks,' replied Neera, massaging her temples with her fingertips. 'How long will it take us from here?'

'Another ten minutes before we reach Hauz Khas.'

Neera looked back at the driver. He was undeniably attractive. Whatever he said, his chest was still bulging. His light beard only added to his allure. She really shouldn't have had that sixth glass of wine.

'You know, madamji, I rarely come to this part of the city, the Hauz Khas area,' Chandar interrupted her reverie.

'Why is that?'

'Because of the Hauz Khas village. Particularly at night. Sometimes drunken girls get into cabs or are dumped inside by their equally drunk friends. They can't even say their own names, let alone the name of the location where they must be dropped. Some of them even puke in the car. Such a mess! I hate them. I recall a girl who abused her mother over the phone because she had stopped a boy from calling her. The dirtiest abuses,' he chuckled, before adding, 'Even I can't say them. She was obviously drunk.'

Neera shifted in her seat. She had the impression he could see right through her; that the insinuation was directed at her. Did he realize she was also drunk?

'It gets awkward for me. Some of them invite me to their homes,' Chandar continued. 'They claim they do not have the exact change. I never go anywhere. I am aware it's a trap. They are drunk right now, but once the alcohol wears off, I could be labelled a rapist and put behind bars. No way, *bhaiya*! Now I have a policy of never, ever getting out of the car.'

Her surroundings were starting to look familiar by this point. She knew she was only a few minutes away from home, which comforted her in an odd way.

'These girls and the *habshis* are two types of passengers I don't like,' Chandar said.

'Habshis?' Neera frowned.

'Yes, you know, the Black people. I can't understand a word they say. One time, a Black man got into the car and refused to pay because he thought I had run the metre twice. How is that even possible? Thank god the other passengers helped him understand.'

Koel, her stepdaughter, had surprised her with a visit last Diwali. She said she was in India for a work project. Neera never asked too many questions about Koel's work, wary of coming across as intrusive, especially since she wasn't particularly interested in the first place. Looking at her photos on Facebook occasionally was enough to reassure Neera of Koel's well-being. She knew the girl was content where she was, and that was all that mattered. It had been a while since Koel had moved to California.

When she found out about Koel's visit, she prepared *chakolis* – the only deep-fried snack Koel could never turn down. But Neera could tell Koel was uneasy from the moment she walked into the house. She barely spoke, which was unusual for her. Neera was aware Koel was not as effusive as her father, but she was never impolite. There was an unspoken contract of civility between the two of them, which they adhered to even after Kishor's death. Thanks to her mother, she was a well-raised girl.

But by the end of the visit, Neera could not stop herself from asking. She knew how sensitive the people of this generation were about their personal space. 'Is everything all right, Koel?' Neera asked cautiously as she handed her the box of chakolis. 'Do you wish to say anything? I want you to know there is nothing you can't tell me that you would tell your Baba.'

Koel gazed at the box in her hands. 'You didn't have to do this,' she said. Her naturally Maharashtrian accent combined with her newly acquired foreign accent made her sound slightly comical. 'But thanks a tonne. I love your chakolis. Mine are never as crisp.' She gave her a warm smile. 'Neeru aunty, I have decided to marry.'

A few odd seconds of silence followed as Koel studied Neera's face for a reaction.

'Oh! That's ... that's fantastic news. Is that why you've come here, then? Is he a Delhi boy? What does he do for a living?'

'He is not from Delhi, Neeru aunty. He is not Indian.'

This revelation came as no surprise to Neera. Koel had been living abroad for four years, and she was likely to stay there, so marrying someone from there made sense. Kishor, Neera imagined, would have definitely grumbled and acted paternal. But she knew she could have calmed him down in minutes.

She took Koel's hands in hers. 'It makes no difference whether you marry an American or an Indian. I am all for it if he makes you happy. White bread or brown bread!' Neera chuckled. She hoped Koel would laugh as well but was disappointed when she did not. She reasoned that these American-types were thin-skinned when it came to jokes, and said: 'I am sorry ... I didn't intend to ... All I was trying to say was ...'

'Oh, no ... aunty, that's fine. It's just that—' Koel paused before saying, 'the bread is not white.'

Neera couldn't follow. Had she misinterpreted the joke? Was she under the impression they were discussing bread? But she was a bright young lady.

Koel took her phone from her handbag and asked Neera if the Wi-Fi was working. She nodded, puzzled, as she watched Koel dial a number.

'Hi Adam! Honey, you remember what I told you about Neera aunty? Right ... she is sitting next to me. I just told her about our wedding, and she is ecstatic. I want to introduce you to her, so I am gonna put the call on video ... okay?' She tapped the phone twice and turned it around to face Neera.

'Neera aunty, this is Adam, my fiancé. Adam, this is Neera aunty ...'

Neera saw an African American man grinning and waving at her from the screen. 'Hi Mrs Dhawan!' he said, his voice heavy. 'How are you doing? It's great to finally see you. Koel was correct. You are absolutely stunning!'

'This lane or the next?' Chandar asked.

'What?'

'Which lane, madam: this one or the next?'

'This one. Just drive straight,' Neera returned to the present. 'I am sorry, I was just thinking about my daughter and son-in-law. He is such a sweetheart.'

'You have a daughter, madam?'

'Yes and no.'

Chandar smiled and frowned at once. His grin made her smile.

'I mean, she is my stepdaughter. You see, my late husband's daughter.'

'Oh! And your husband is ...'

'Yes, it has been four years. That's it, pull over, we've arrived.'

The car came to a stop. A stray dog a few metres away barked once to acknowledge their presence before ducking its head again. Neera looked around. She was on her own territory. The profound sense of security she felt mingled with the wine-induced recklessness in her mind, forming a potent cocktail.

'It must be difficult for a woman like you to handle everything on your own in this city,' he observed. His hand accidentally brushed against hers. She let her shawl slide off.

'You know, Chandar …' Neera locked her eyes with him, hitting him with a brilliant smile. 'You are correct. It can be lonely sometimes. And Delhi is a dangerous city.'

'I see what you mean, madam.' Chandar stumbled. She could tell her smile had hit its target.

'I wish I had more friends,' she whispered. 'Friends like *you*.'

Chandar gaped at her.

'Unfortunately, your policy stands in our way. I am sure you never get out of the car. If you did, I would let you do things you haven't done in a long time.' She pinched his cheek and handed him a 500-rupee note.

'The fare is just 350, madam.'

'Keep the change. And by the way, if you want to come upstairs, I have a task for you. I'm going to brew some tea. For two people. I live on the third floor, in case you change your mind,' Neera said, without breaking eye contact with him. She got out of the car and gently shut the door before walking away.

She was certain he would follow. She was still convinced after nearly ten minutes.

Chandar discovered the door ajar. He walked in and saw Neera standing at the end of the corridor. It seemed to lead to the drawing room.

'I suppose I can make an exception tonight, madam,' he admitted softly.

'Welcome,' said Neera, smiling, as she turned.

When Chandar entered the drawing room, a couple were sitting on the sofa.

'Chandar, please meet my daughter Koel and my son-in-law Adam. Guys, this is Chandar, my friend who drove me home. He usually doesn't drive women from Hauz Khas and Black people, but he has agreed to make an exception for me tonight. As a result, he will drive you to the airport. Isn't that thoughtful of him? Now hurry up and get your luggage before Chandar and I finish our tea.'

Score

'WHICH PERFUME ARE you wearing today?' Anirban asked his wife. The earth beneath their feet was still damp. The sun had been sickly when the day began but it gathered vigour as it clambered up the sky. By noon, it shone so brightly that it coaxed the couple out of the hotel for a stroll. There was a vast open space outside the hotel, fringed by chinar, deodar and poplar trees, along which flowed a rivulet. It had been Aditi's decision to come to Kashmir for their second anniversary. Anirban wanted a beach holiday, but for some reason, Aditi had been drawn to Kashmir.

After many failed attempts to dissuade her, Anirban had given up. Very early on in their marriage, he had realized that arguing with Aditi was as difficult as loving her. Their match had been orchestrated by Aditi's mother, Paromita, who had created her profile on a matrimonial website.

They had met only thrice before deciding to say *yes*. Aditi was not averse to the idea of marriage or settling down. But initially she had found the idea of matchmaking on the matrimonial website tame and boring. Choosing this path, she thought, could make her susceptible to being called conventional.

Growing up, Aditi had believed her partner would be the result of a fortuitous discovery and not a tedious search. She had thought she would *run into* her life partner someday, somewhere. Maybe she would begin a conversation with someone reading the same book as hers on a metro (she never took the reserved coach) after being amazed at their similar taste in books and music. Or maybe someday someone would stop by to admire the roses and gardenias that she had painstakingly cultivated on one end of the small porch in her flat; she would perhaps then thank that person for the compliment and invite him indoors for a glass of lemonade; maybe he would agree, and they would have the most delightful conversation over lemonade; maybe the rather plain-looking man would actually turn out to be the CEO of a large firm; they would frequently meet over some more lemonade, fall in love and subsequently get married.

But her fanciful notions began fragmenting with every passing year in her twenties. She wasn't a girl anymore; she was a grown-up woman with standards. An article on 'Idea Catalog', a blog she chanced upon, confirmed this. As she began to read more and more of such blogs, she grew certain that being single was not her fault. They assured her that she was single because love was overrated, because others were shallow, because she knew *her worth*. That there was nothing wrong with her, except her *uniqueness* and *individuality*, which she must guard most fiercely, even at the expense of love.

Whatever the reason, after entering her thirties, she started to travel in the metro coach reserved for ladies. She no longer grubbed out the weeds from her pots on the same day she spotted them and with as much aggression. She started waiting for the weekend to prune the plants. Slowly, she began to relent to her mother's pursuit of her marriage. Humouring her mother stopped seeming like a bizarre idea. 'The steep slope that joins the elevated fancy to ground reality is dangerously slippery – a nudge in the form of persuasion or the passage of time is all it takes to trigger the descent,' her mother would say. Aditi was on her way down.

By the time Anirban's proposal came her way, things had taken a turn for the worse. Her father had been ill for some time. Aditi had grown tired of being held responsible by her mother for his illness. 'I am not saying he's ill because of you; I am just saying he will either recover or will at least pass away peacefully once he sees you married. And that's not too much to ask after all he has done for you. Look at Kishor uncle. He couldn't even live to see his daughter finish her course in America. Who can predict life!' Her mother had once told her in a heated exchange of words. She knew she was being emotionally manipulated, but she relented, nonetheless. She, too, was fed up of the hunt that had been going on for almost two years. She wanted to focus on work, and she told herself and her friends that the arranged marriage route was nothing other than outsourcing. It saved her time, and she could assign blame to the third party if the project failed. And Anirban wasn't an unattractive proposal. He too, like her, wanted to get married soon. Their marriage was an outcome of 'search fatigue', she often quipped.

'The fragrance is really nice, isn't it? It was lying unused in my vanity case all this while. The brand has a fancy French name I cannot pronounce right for the life of me. Neera aunty gave it to me as our wedding present,' she said, hooking her arm around his. 'Along with the air-fryer, of course,' she added quickly. Anirban gave her a look that said he couldn't care less even if she had gifted them nothing. Aditi smiled awkwardly at her faux pas.

'You remember Neera aunty from the wedding? Our old neighbour?'

'The sexy aunty?'

'Yes, yes ... that's her.' She smiled.

Aditi had full, thick lips; a feature Anirban found attractive in women. He repressed an urge to cup her breasts at this moment and squeeze them like the previous night. He knew she loved it.

'She is a sweetheart. She was excellent at teaching maths. She and Kishor uncle lived next door,' Aditi said. It seemed as if she was talking to herself. 'Kishor uncle had a daughter, Koel, who used to be a friend. Ma used her example to convince me to get married. She lives in the States now.'

'Her example?'

'Her father died before she got married. It happened suddenly. You know my mother, she milked the episode along with Papa's deteriorating health, which made it worse.'

But Anirban wasn't paying attention, she noticed. He leaned in as if to whisper something in her ear and inhaled deeply.

'Hmm ... lovely scent. Thank the sexy aunty for me,' he said.

'Were you eying her, you perv?'

He shrugged. 'She was pretty – you can't deny that.'

'Men!' Aditi sighed in mock anger.

'Oh, come on! Like you have stopped checking out men?

I caught you ogling at our Kashmiri hotel manager. What is his name? Akash?'

'Akshay,' Aditi corrected him.

'Akshay – Akash – whatever!' Anirban said. 'Do you want to take him home?'

'He looks like a fluffy rabbit, doesn't he? The kind who would get sullied simply by breathing in the polluted air of the city. Or maybe he will melt in Delhi's blistering heat? So no! I am going to enjoy him while I am here,' she said, winking at him.

Anirban was not used to the kind of bluntness that Aditi very generously demonstrated. It made him uneasy, more so because it came from a woman. He had had many forthright women friends, but this was his wife: Mrs Anirban Bhattacharya. But over the past two years of marriage, he had understood perfectly well she would not change her behaviour, not for him at any rate. So now he tried to conceal his uneasiness in a smirk or a shrug whenever he could, and when he could not, a nasty argument ensued.

'Let's sit there for a while,' said Anirban, pointing to a tree stump.

Pahalgam was beautiful. But it hadn't matched Anirban's expectations. They were told this was the first time it had not snowed this time of the year. The last snow had fallen about two weeks ago; usually at this time, the place was covered under a thick blanket of snow, as their slender-nosed, pink-cheeked hotel manager had told him on their arrival. Secretly, Anirban had felt vindicated. It wasn't his idea to come here after all. And knowing his wife's impatient nature he was sure she would want to go back, now that it wasn't snowing. But she did not.

'Where do I sit?' she asked when she saw him march towards the stump.

Anirban glanced around: there were patches of snow on the ground from the last time it had snowed. They looked like the suds of shaving foam he often left on the bathroom floor after shaving. Thank God Aditi could not whine about these, at least.

'It's big enough for two, you know. Or you could just sit on my lap,' he said.

Aditi looked around. There was no one to be seen. She sat on his thigh, looping her arm around his neck. Instantly, she felt a sense of discomfort that wasn't purely physical.

'I'd rather sit here,' she said awkwardly, moving next to him after a minute. But before that they had to take a customary selfie.

She sat on the edge of the stump. The sunlight sieving through the cluster of leaves wove an exquisite pattern around them. Though it wasn't snowing, it was cold enough even at this hour of noon for her to be greedy for sun. Sunshine glazed her body like a thick layer of the golden pineapple jam her mother used to spread on her toast when she was young. Anirban was squinting, she saw. Why could he never enjoy anything fully? Throughout the flight from Delhi to Srinagar, he had complained about the long stop-over at Jammu; he found the *rogan josh* she had ordered for the both of them too rich and oily, and the pashmina she had bought for his mother was nice but a shade too light. Nothing was wholly delightful for him. There was always a *but.*

'Did you speak to Ma about the party?' she asked, untying her muffler.

'No. What am I to say to her? It's their fortieth wedding anniversary, the first big event we are hosting after our wedding, and their daughter-in-law will skip it. I still think it's unfair,' Anirban said. He spoke with measured nonchalance as if her absence wouldn't matter to him at all, as if he was only concerned about his parents' feelings. Internally, he was livid. After several arguments over the matter, she did not know any other way to handle this other than saying, 'Please don't make it more difficult than it has to be. It is my work. You know I tried hard to reschedule, but it didn't work out. I will speak with Ma and Baba myself, I guess.'

There! She took it upon herself again. Aditi: the doer, the go-getter, the agenda-setter. Like she always did. Even in bed. She would touch herself even when they were fucking, making him feel insufficient.

'Well, you could. And see what they have to say,' Anirban said, standing up and yawning. 'I feel like taking a nap. Would they have fixed the heater by now? You asked your Akash guy to get it fixed, right?'

'*Akshay*!' hissed Aditi, producing the same sound she had made that morning on biting into a crisp, golden Kashmiri apple. She raised her arm lazily for him to grab.

Anirban had not liked their hotel either. He wanted to stay at one of the cosy cottages on the other side of the rivulet. They looked natural and budget-friendly. But then Aditi had planned and managed the whole trip. The destination, duration, accommodation – everything was of her choosing.

'Yeah ... yeah ... Akash – Akshay, it's all the same,' Anirban said and kissed her as if to stake a claim.

Ravens cawed from the top of the trees and the air was

dense with the scent of pinecones as they walked back to the resort, holding hands.

'I wonder if this Akshay guy was the reason you planned the whole trip,' Anirban said. '*Badi kutti cheez ho tum.*'

Aditi giggled.

While in the afternoon, Aditi had praised the manager's looks simply to tease her husband, later that evening, she realized why her husband was jealous. They were dining in the hall where Akshay, the manager, was overseeing things. He was personally ensuring that all the guests were being served properly. Aditi wondered if she was the only one overwhelmed by his beauty.

Perhaps he had caught Aditi stealing glances at him. He walked up to their table and shook hands with them warmly. When the manager asked if the service was satisfactory, Anirban brought up the issue with their room heater to Aditi's chagrin. She cut in to say that it was fixed now, and that they liked the hotel. Anirban gave her a look.

'I apologize for the inconvenience, sir,' Akshay said sincerely.

'Oh, that's alright,' Anirban said as he patted the young man's back. 'We like it here.' He didn't have any real complaint. He just wanted to provoke his wife.

'That's nice of you to say. I should make up for it, nevertheless. Allow me to offer our finest wine to the lovely lady,' Akshay said.

'That's not needed, Mister Manager, thank you,' Aditi said,

looking at her husband, implicitly urging him to join her in saying no.

'Why not? I think that's a great idea.' Anirban smirked.

'Please, ma'am. Have it, I insist. It's on the house,' said Akshay.

'On one condition, though,' Anirban chimed in.

Both his wife and the manager looked at him curiously.

'We will accept it only if you join us for some drinks,' Anirban said.

Akshay laughed softly and said, 'Thank you, but I don't wish to disturb you. I will send for the wine.'

Aditi noticed that his eyes twinkled under the glow of the overhead lamp. 'Please, Mister Manager, join us – we insist,' she said.

'You are not intruding, believe me. We have had an overdose of each other.' Anirban winked at her. 'Can I get some rum for myself, though?'

'Sure.' The manager called for the drinks and joined their table.

Over the course of the conversation, they learned that he had a degree in hospitality from Penrith and had interned in Australia for a year before moving back to Kashmir. When she asked the reason for his return to what could, at best, be described as a 'volatile environment', he suddenly became pensive and, after a meaningful pause, said, 'This is where my heart is, you see.' With flowy hair, gentle eyes and a quiet attitude, in that moment, he could well have been a subject banished from a Renaissance painting.

He talked to them about his growing-up years in the valley and the exodus that followed. His family was originally from

Pampore, where they used to own two orchards of saffron. They lived in Delhi now.

'Do you remember all of it?'

'Very vaguely. I was young. Mostly, I've heard stories from my parents.'

'Do they visit you?' Aditi asked in a dewy voice.

'No, they don't. They just won't come here,' Akshay said. He set his elbows on the table, locking his fingers, and rested his chin on them. 'I go to Delhi, though.'

'Delhi? How often?' she asked, her eyes bright with excitement. Anirban coughed.

'Once in two months, I guess,' Akshay said, looking into his glass of wine as if hoping to find something there. 'My parents want me to move out of here. Their wounds are still fresh. Whenever I visit them, my mother asks, "Are there not enough five-star hotels in Delhi, Mumbai or Chandigarh?"'

'You know you could act or model for a living in Mumbai too – you're a good-looking man,' Anirban said as he refilled Aditi's glass. 'And I'm sure Wifey will second me on this.'

She knew her husband was itching for her to speak. Aditi sipped some wine before saying, 'I endorse that. You are very handsome.'

She had learned to deny her husband the perverse pleasure of humiliating her. Aditi knew how desperately he sought these moments, but by now, she had mastered the art of foiling his attempts. She had started to see it as a game between them and had begun keeping a score mentally. Last time he had scored on her, making her reveal her true age to his boss, because the man had assumed she was five years younger. There were no ill feelings; it was just a game.

Akshay chuckled. It was clear from his body language that he was used to receiving compliments on his looks. 'I act almost on a daily basis. I just don't get paid for it.' He paused to glance at Aditi before raising his glass with a smile. 'Or maybe I do.'

Aditi was intrigued. Or maybe she was just tired of the familiarity that had grown like moss between her and Anirban. There was nothing new to be discovered about her husband. And what she didn't know about him, he would never reveal to her, she could sense. Whereas this man, drinking wine across the table from her with a glint of mischief in his eyes, was like fresh snow to her.

'Do you have a girlfriend? Or a wife?' Anirban asked, taking another sip.

Aditi saw Akshay's cheek turn a deeper shade of pink as he shook his head.

'Why not?' she cut in.

'Women are boring,' Akshay said casually. She cocked an eyebrow at him.

'Or maybe I haven't found someone like you yet,' he added with a smile, catching her off guard.

She instantly looked around at Anirban to see if he had registered the remark.

'Oh! You can have her if you want because you won't find another one like her,' her husband laughed loudly. She sensed he was drunk.

The bitter wine was starting to taste sweet now, diluted by their host's lively sense of humour and charm. For the first time on the trip, she saw Anirban laughing freely. She reached for his hand under the table and clasped it. He, in turn, looked into her eyes and smiled.

'Let's go now; it's late. Mister Manager must be tired,' she said, beaming at Akshay. 'Remember, *we* are on vacation, not he.'

'Of course!' said Anirban, reaching for a glass of water. 'I'll just use the loo and be back.'

Aditi gave him a look that said, *you could pee upstairs; you're drunk.*

'I'm fine. I'll just be a minute, darling,' said Anirban, kissing her head before he shuffled away. She thought she saw Akshay's face twitch for a split second when Anirban kissed her. Maybe she was reading too much into it. Perhaps he wasn't used to such an open display of affection. Perhaps his Australian days were very long gone, and he had pruned them in his memory to retain only the parts that could withstand Kashmir's cold.

There was an awkward silence between the two of them when Anirban was gone. Aditi picked up her phone from the table and tapped it for no apparent reason.

'How long have you been married?' Akshay asked to fill the silence.

Aditi was forced to put her phone down. 'It's our second anniversary next month. I have to travel on account of work then, so we are celebrating it in advance.'

'No wonder you still look like a couple very much in love,' he said, smiling. She couldn't make out if it was a smile or a smirk, but she smiled back.

'Lilac looks perfect on you, I think,' he said, the smile still lingering around his lips. Aditi would have left by now if it hadn't been for his slender nose and rose-tinted cheeks. Anirban never paid her any such compliment. He never bothered noticing which colour suited her the best. She too never expected that from him, really – she was a career woman after all – but at that moment, she was forced to accept that it wasn't all that bad to be appreciated for things other than those that could be tabulated in a Microsoft Excel sheet. Or was it the way he said it?

'Thank you!' She tried to look away.

'Isn't he gone a long time? Should I go and check in on him?' he enquired.

'Would you? It would be kind of you. We have to head to Gulmarg tomorrow morning. For skiing, you know. I want to start early.'

He moved past the other tables and guests with the gait of a dancer, smiling and nodding at them.

The two men emerged soon, Akshay holding Anirban's left arm.

'Package delivered, madam,' he said upon reaching the table.

'Oh, am I now a package? Must be handled with care, eh?' Anirban laughed.

Aditi stood up. 'Thanks a lot, Mister Manager. You've been a great company. Excuse us now. Good night.' She turned to her husband to grab the same arm that Akshay had released. 'Let's go ... shall we?'

'The pleasure was mine, ma'am.' He half-bowed. 'Should I escort you two to the room? He's a bit ... you know,' he whispered in her ears.

'I am fine. Absolutely fine. Don't behave like Aditi!' Anirban said, surprising them both.

'We are fine, thank you. Good night,' she repeated.

As they walked towards the elevator, she turned around and saw him watching them get on. He had the same ambiguous expression on his face when she had asked why he had returned to Kashmir. As if he was hiding something. Anirban could never do that. He could never, for instance, hide his resentment about her foreign work trip next month, no matter how unaffected he pretended to be.

'Are you okay? You've had too much to drink.'

'I'm fine, baby,' Anirban said, bending forward to kiss her. She averted the kiss.

'Let's just sleep tonight. We have an early start tomorrow,' Aditi said. Her mind was elsewhere.

Within minutes of entering the room, she realized she had left her phone on the table downstairs. Anirban had already collapsed on the bed with his shoes on. She'd have to go get the phone on her own.

When she reached the table, she caught a bit of fright because she couldn't see the phone. Had it been stolen? Oh, no … there it was, hidden beneath a napkin. She sighed and picked it up. As she turned, she stepped on a tissue with something scribbled on it. Once she was sure no one around was looking, she swiftly retrieved the crumpled tissue.

The note said: *Meet me in room number 101. Tomorrow. 11 a.m.*

She looked for Akshay. He was nowhere to be seen. There were hardly any occupied tables now. A couple of waiters were purveying food to the few that were. She slipped the tissue in her handbag and went back.

The next morning Anirban woke up with a hangover, and Aditi with a dilemma. She had spent all night thinking about the message, partly hoping that it wasn't meant for her and partly hoping that it was. She had thought that the message would fade away by the morning like a vague, absurd dream. But she had forgotten that while sleep can perhaps mitigate the sense of guilt, it cannot wipe out its physical evidence. The message still sat in her handbag, limp and creased, like her conscience.

The handbag was right next to Anirban on the side table. She looked at it sneakily, desperate to remove it from his reach. She was being silly, of course. Why would he open her handbag, that too in her presence? She was thinking too much. She could discard the message or bring it to Anirban's notice.

No, that wasn't a good idea. He would only make the matters worse by raising hell. She wanted to safeguard the serene mood of this trip and this place at all costs. She was capable of dealing with this on her own. Maybe she could write to the owners of the luxury hotel chain directly, or she could tweet about this – Anirban wasn't on Twitter, after all – and call out the hotel on social media. Or she could give this man a piece of her mind herself. This ridiculously good-looking man with a slender nose and puddles of kindness for eyes, who warmly smiled at them whenever he ran into them in the lobby. All of this confusion was making her head spin as well. But unlike her husband, she couldn't complain about it or use it as an excuse to not go skiing in Gulmarg.

'What do you mean you don't want to go? Don't be a spoilsport, please. Have some coffee, and you'll be fine,' she scowled.

'My head is splitting,' Anirban mumbled, with his face pressed against the pillow and his arm resting on her breasts. 'It's dreadful. Maybe your Mister Manager spiked my drink last night.'

She pushed his arm away with a jerk and nearly howled, 'Don't be stupid! Just get up and get ready. The taxi will be here in thirty minutes.'

'Why are you being such a bitch? I have a headache, I can't go.' His volume increased. The friction wasn't new for them, nor its outcome. Anirban knew she wouldn't change their plan once she'd made up her mind. She had planned to go skiing. With or without him.

'Fine then, rot here all day. I am going.'

He watched her get dressed from the bed, wondering if she had brought him along on this trip only because an anniversary trip without a husband wouldn't make sense; if he was needed any more than the boarding pass she had kept in her handbag at the airport; and if once they had reached their destination, he would be neglected or thrown away for all she cared. He felt an absurd need to find out if the boarding pass was still in her bag.

She caught him staring at her in the mirror as she tied her hair into a ponytail. Why did he have to be such a killjoy all the time? She wanted to ski. The weather forecast for the next day was unfavourable for an outing. Wait, what was he doing? Was he reaching for her handbag?

Aditi sprang to her feet, almost pouncing on her handbag. 'What do you want?'

'The boarding pass ... I wanted to see if we still have it.' He said aloud.

'The boarding pass? Are you still fucking drunk?'

'There's no need to be so shrill. It's just a boarding pass, not your salary slip.'

'For God's sake, Anirban, get up and take a shower.'

Before he could think of a rejoinder, the phone in the room rang.

'Your cab is here apparently, your highness.'

Aditi felt a pang of sympathy, looking at his face. She should not have reacted so harshly.

'I'll have them send you coffee and breakfast. You should take a shower and step out for a while. Take a walk, maybe; it's sunny outside. You will feel better.' She kissed his forehead and hugged him lightly. 'I will miss you.'

Anirban shrugged. Swallowing the words that had risen to his lips, he said, 'Will miss you too.'

As Aditi walked through the lobby, her eyes searched for Akshay. She was still a little jittery from the handbag episode. She couldn't see him anywhere. Was he evading her now?

She enquired about him at the front desk.

'He is off duty today, ma'am. He must be in his room. Mr Khalid is in charge of things today. Would you like to talk to him if you have some concern?' said the boy at the reception.

'No ... no concern. Never mind, thank you. Could you please send some black coffee and sandwiches to room 218?'

In the cab, Aditi smiled at the other tourists from the hotel, who were accompanying her to Gulmarg. She plugged in her earphones to avoid small talk.

Among her co-passengers was a couple, obviously newly married – going from the thick red bangles on the woman's wrists – and three young men, apparently rich and college-going. They looked too optimistic to be anything else. The couple was clicking selfies in the cab and the youngsters were howling enthusiastically as the car began moving. She wondered if the couple was truly in love, and if the bunch of friends was really as enthusiastic.

What if Anirban had seen the tissue? How would she have explained it? Was it just a drunken mistake on Akshay's part? Perhaps, the message wasn't even meant for her. It could have been lying on the floor before they took the table; she might not have noticed it. But what about all the flirtatious feelers he'd been sending her that Anirban had been too drunk to notice. Or maybe he did notice. Could that have been something Anirban desired? Why not – it would give him something to use against her for the rest of her life if an argument turned bitter. What an absurd thought that was!

She looked out of the window to distract herself, taking in the scenic beauty. A chain of hills in the background rolled parallel to the road. The more distant, snow-covered ones looked like massive mounds of vanilla sprinkled with chocolate-chips.

Her attempts at distraction failed. Pulling out the tissue from her handbag, she stared at it for a while. Then she asked the driver to stop the cab saying she wanted to go back. She made up a lie about being pregnant and feeling sick. No one could object now. They hadn't come very far in any case.

After reaching the hotel, she crept inside, looking around watchfully. She found herself in the grip of something beyond herself while swiftly making her way to room number 101. How should they proceed? Would he ask awkward questions about her marriage? What would she use as an excuse for this blunder? She was content in her marriage. It was not perfect, of course. But then, which marriage was? She had never expected much from it. She had got married because she had to. And because Baba had been very ill. Also, there was nothing wrong with Anirban – he was simply peevish, as she had discovered after their marriage. Did that make matters worse?

Perhaps, she was just curious. Could curiosity be a good enough reason? Maybe Akshay would not ask her questions. Maybe he would just grab her and undress her without saying a word. How would his soft lips feel against her navel? How would his stubble feel against her face? Shouldn't she ask him if he's done something like this before? She couldn't possibly be the only one. It seemed highly unethical. Had she read about such an incident on Facebook, she too would have been outraged. But she continued walking towards the room.

She knocked on the door, oblivious to any sound other than of her wildly beating heart. There was no response. She rang the bell this time – still nothing.

She reached for the bell again, but was unable to press it. Just as she decided to retreat, someone from the housekeeping staff passed by with a trolley full of fresh white towels and toiletries, almost startling her. Averting her eyes, she dashed to the elevator.

Her heart thumped against her chest, yet there was a strange relief; she was thankful the door had not opened. She had not experienced this rush in a very long while. Now that it had subsided, she was able to think more clearly. This is what excited her – the surge of passion coursing from her head to toe, the chilling anticipation of the next moment and the frisson of unpredictability.

The message must have been for someone else, she thought. It was silly to think a cultured man like Akshay would behave in such a manner. She decided to go back and apologize to Anirban – for being rude, for leaving him alone, for being herself. They could have lunch by the riverside, just as he wanted. Perhaps they could even move to one of those cottages for the last two days of their trip, even if it meant she had to cook. No, she doubled back, maybe that was too much. But they must go for lunch.

She turned the key gently, taking care not to startle him.

As she entered the room quietly, she was stunned to discover that Anirban had scored yet again. Lying in bed with him was Akshay, naked, caressing Anirban's hairy chest. The message, it struck her, had not been intended for her indeed.

Tonight, I sit once again to unload the squalor of my thoughts onto this paper. Must the paper not resent me?

Not all of that squalor comes through. Some of it is filtered by codes of propriety while the rest by the subconscious, shuddering at the prospect of revealing it. There are things that refuse to get impressed upon this blank page; they will continue to gnaw at me from within. Vices, too, seek company. By setting them out here, by letting them take shape of intelligible words, I could have allowed the vices to find their kin that reside in other souls who might chance upon such mindless scribbling.

'Oh! That happens to you too!'

'Damn! I know that feeling!' Everyone would have exclaimed as their eyes read about my vices and my lapses in judgement. It could have lessened someone's burden of shame, or made someone feel only human, more human. It could have given someone a sense of belonging, a sense of commonality, so they feel less isolated. But I deny them this experience.

A strange fear restrains me. It is the same fear that keeps one from stepping out of the house without wearing clothes. Call it shame, if you must, but it is a fear. Our vices, however universal, have some distinct flavour that manifests uniquely. We wonder if this distinctiveness singles us out, making a spectacle out of us, or if it would earn us the disregard of people we love – but mostly, and sadly, the people who do not care for our existence.

The fear remains: What if they use it against us at a later date? What if we are only seen through the prism of such revelations, our every action judged in the light of confessions. We tell ourselves that the vices are ours, they are not us in their entirety. What we call 'us' is but a sum of the vices and virtues. Riddled with all such deliberations, the mind rules against letting the filth flow unfettered.

It's that time of the night again when I sit to unload my thoughts onto a fresh page. Must this page not resent me?

April Fool

All my friends have siblings. My mummy and papa also have siblings. Pranav mama, Mummy's brother, had called last night. I love talking to him but when I asked him why I didn't have a brother, he told me to hand over the phone to Mummy. I handed her the phone, waiting for their chat to end as I wanted to play games on it. My father has installed 'Angry Birds' on Mummy's mobile phone for me. But Mummy sounded upset after she hung up.

Today, I asked her why she sounded sad last night. She didn't tell me why, saying I am too young to understand. She had said the same thing when I asked her why I don't have a sibling. When will she understand I am eight years old now? I understand things. Like I know Papa and she have been having problems since Nilu, the young girl, started living with us. They mostly argue at night, thinking I am asleep. But I am not. I only shut my eyes. Sometimes, I really fall asleep, and miss their arguments. A lot changes when I sleep: Time jumps; within seconds, the next day begins and Mummy wakes me up for school again. I don't like to sleep. Nowadays, Nilu wakes me up. 'Baba, baba ...' she calls out, in between giggles for no reason. She giggles constantly. When I asked Mummy why Nilu giggles all the time, she said it's because Nilu is sad. What kind of person giggles when they are sad? Mummy gives the same reply she does for almost all my questions: 'You are too young to understand, Manu.'

I think she is dumb, this girl, Nilu. Mummy says she is a year older than me, but I don't believe her. When I asked her which April Fools' prank I should play this time, she giggled again. She doesn't know what April Fool is. Isn't that dumb for a girl her age?

We had found her in Delhi last year when we visited my nani's house for the summer vacation. We go there every year. Along with her father, Nilu used to sell vegetables down the road from my nani's house. I had seen Mummy observing her many times when we went out to buy milk and bread. We always saw her from a distance, though. In Mumbai, we buy groceries from the mall. I hate the queues there. People buy a lot of stuff that takes really long to get billed. They don't need most of it. I know that because we too buy a lot of things we do not need. Except the vegetables.

Once, when it was just about to rain, Mummy decided to go up to the vegetable stall and asked Nilu her name. With big, bulging eyes, Nilu was dark and shabby-looking. I mean, she is still dark and has big eyes. Really big eyes. Or maybe her tiny face makes her eyes look even bigger. When Mummy asked if she went to school, Nilu laughed out loud. I couldn't tell what she had found funny. She looked around like she was searching for someone else to join her in the laugh. I've usually seen grown-ups do this; whenever they find something funny or exciting, they look for someone else to share a laugh with or give them a high-five. Papa does that when he watches cricket on TV. Nilu is quite strange; she often does things that other girls her age don't, not in my school at least. Her laughter at Mummy's question distracted the man in the stall next to hers, who was trying hard to cover his fruits with a plastic sheet. It was windy.

'*Main school nahi jaati, didi,*' she said and continued to laugh. When Mummy asked why she does not go to school, she replied that her father would beat her to a pulp. '*Maal kaun bechega? Tera baap?*' she said, mimicking her father. Then she said something I can't remember. I think she mentioned that her father hits her. But the stupid girl kept laughing.

I didn't find it funny, neither did my mother. Papa never hits me. Once, when he had yelled at me, he and Mummy had a huge fight. Now, my mother just stood there, staring at Nilu blankly. I couldn't tell if she was scared or stunned, but she didn't look amused. It began to rain. Like it always does – slowly at first, a drop here, a drop there and then fast-fast. No, that's how it rains in Delhi. Here in Mumbai, it rains in one go – now it's not raining and the next minute, it is all rain and rain. Mummy clutched my hand and dragged me away. We ran back to Nani's house.

That was our first encounter with Nilu. Soon, I forgot about her. I had to teach Nani how to watch videos on YouTube. Nani is really slow and she doesn't know how to handle touch-screen phones. She is funny: she keeps asking me what will happen if she accidentally presses all the buttons on the screen while using the phone.

Two days later, when we went to the market again, Mummy saw Nilu with her parents. She asked me to wait at a little distance from their stall because she wanted to speak with Nilu's mummy. She asked me not to go out of sight, not even for a second or I wouldn't get any ice cream. I wanted ice cream so I didn't move. I saw her talking to Nilu's parents. Nilu's mummy was as dark as her. She too had big eyes but she didn't speak much. It was mostly Nilu's papa who was talking. He looked angry while Nilu looked confused (nothing new!). She hid behind her mother, but I saw her peering at me from there with those big eyes.

When Mummy came back, I asked her why that man was yelling at her. She said he was ill, and she had asked him to get treated. What's wrong in that? I asked. 'Maybe he does not like injections like me which is why he was angry.' 'Maybe!' Mummy said and kissed me.

I heard her discussing Nilu with Nana and Nani while I was watching *Doraemon*. I couldn't understand why she was so taken with Nilu. Nana told her nothing could be done unless the parents agreed to send the girl to school. They couldn't be forced. Nani said we should offer them money, to which my mummy said Nilu's papa would use it to buy alcohol. Some people do that, I have seen that on television. They drink alcohol and create mess. They are bad people. I think Nilu's papa is also a bad man. He looks like them.

After that incident, whenever we crossed Nilu's stall, Mummy would hand something in Nilu's palms. Ice cream, chocolate, biscuits, those things. Nilu hadn't shown any good behaviour; she still got the goodies. I get goodies only when Mummy is happy with me or when I show good behaviour or if I get an A+ on my tests. When I asked Mummy why she buys goodies for Nilu, Mummy said she will buy me goodies too. But that did not answer my question. Anyway, I got the goodies, so I did not care.

Nani often complains that I ask too many questions. Mummy tells her it is a good sign, but she doesn't answer all my questions either. Sometimes she just smiles and hugs me big; when she is mad, she asks me more questions in return. 'Have you finished your homework, Manu? Did you keep your toys in place?'

Nilu and Mummy became friends quickly. She would grin and wave at us madly whenever we would pass by in the morning. She would yell, *'Didi, namaste! Didi namaste!'* from across the road and Mummy would smile back, though she had told me yelling on the road is bad manners.

Nilu's mother knew my nani well. Sometimes, since Nani was old, she delivered vegetables to her house. Nani asked her to bring Nilu along to play with me. All the kids here are grown up so I have no friends to play with. Seniors at school – they go for tuition classes in the evening. My nani thought Nilu would be a good companion for me. So, she used to come over in the afternoons. Though I did not know what to do with her – she was girl, not a boy. But we played ludo.

One afternoon, Nilu did not turn up. I started playing with Nanaji when the doorbell rang. I was happy because it meant all the adults would wake up from their nap. All the adults in this flat sleep in the afternoon. I had managed to keep Nana awake and now Nani was awake too. Nani opened the door we saw Nilu standing with her mummy, who was crying loudly. After Nani asked them to come in, they sat down on the floor as Nilu's mother kept crying. She didn't say anything when Nani asked her why she was so upset. No, she said something, but it didn't make sense to us because she was crying. She kept pointing to her daughter. Nilu was standing silently. By then, Mummy came out of bathroom with a towel wrapped around her head. She smells like soap after a bath, my mummy.

She also asked vegetable-seller aunty what had happened. But the woman kept crying. Then she asked Nilu, but she didn't say anything either. The girl's eyes were swollen, and she had blue marks on her face and neck. Nani gave the woman some water to drink and asked her to calm down. Nana looked on, confused, and kept asking, '*Arre, kya ho gaya?*'

After ten minutes, the woman said something to Mummy. I didn't fully understand it but it was about Nilu's father. Maybe he beat up Nilu. That's why there were marks on her body. Mummy's face grew pale and, for few seconds, she could not speak. She whispered something in Nani's ears, at which Nani covered her mouth with her hands. Then Mummy walked over and hugged Nilu. The girl shrank when Mummy touched her. I get upset when my mother cries, so I too started crying. Nilu still stayed quiet. Holding me aside, Nana asked me to go into the room. But I was frozen. I wrapped my hands around Mummy from behind as she hugged Nilu.

Nana explained they would have to file a police complaint. But Nilu had to be rescued, Mummy said. I didn't understand. Nilu hadn't been kidnapped. She was right in front of us. But Mummy kept repeating the same thing.

Mummy and Nana took Nilu and her mother to the police station. While Nani and I would wait for them to return, Mummy asked me to finish my colouring book. My game of ludo was unfinished because of Nilu. I hated her, but I could see she was sad. You cannot hate someone when they are sad.

They came back in an hour, with Nilu. When Nani asked what had happened, Nana asked Mummy to take Nilu inside and give her something to eat. I was filling colours in my book. When Nilu disappeared from the scene, Nana began talking to Nani as though they were planning a prank: 'Vimla backed out at the last moment, right outside the police station. She fell at our feet and started wailing. She said if her husband gets arrested, the landlord will throw her and her children out. She has two more sons, both younger than Nilu. Who will earn the bread for them? Priyanshi tried very hard to convince her that the man is dangerous, but she just wouldn't listen and went on crying. Finally, she had to ask Vimla to send Nilu with us.'

Nani listened quietly. As Nana sat on the sofa and took off his glasses to wipe them, she said meekly, 'Don't you think it's their private matter? That man could be dangerous. What if he harms our Manu to get back at us? We should report this to the police and send the girl back to her mother.' I was scared when I heard my name. I decided to never go down that road ever again. I thought of calling up Papa to come and take me away before the dirty man harmed me because of Nilu.

In the meantime, Mummy returned from the bedroom and said, 'He is a coward, Ma, don't you see? Consumed by alcohol, he harms this little girl and his wife. I could not have let the girl stay in that hell ... I have some friends who work in NGOs that look after children in need of help. I will talk to them.'

'Don't be silly, Priyanshi. You're going back to Mumbai tomorrow. What will we do with this girl here?' Nani scolded

Mummy. Because she is my Mummy's mummy, you know. She also scolds Mummy when she sleeps till late in the morning. Sometimes, when Nana and I come back from the park where he does *pranayam*, I see Mummy still sleeping. She yawns, hides her head under the pillow before raising her head to wink at me. I laugh at her and then run around, hug Mummy and sleep next to her under the quilt. But Nani grumbles and complains that women should not sleep till late. Thank God, I am a boy.

'I don't know, Ma … I will take her with me. I can't let her return to that hellhole,' Mummy said. She looked at Nana for help. But he just shook his head and said, 'Think carefully, Priyanshi. Talk to Manish first.'

Manish is my papa's name. Mr Manish Rohatgi.

That night, nobody said much at the dining table. Nilu was given a plateful of food in our room, where Mummy and I sleep when we are in Delhi. Mummy says she and Pranav mama shared this room when they were kids. Like me. I can't imagine her as a small girl. But I've seen photographs in which Mummy is wearing a frock and Pranav mama is wearing a crown. Mummy still has the frock; she had shown it to me once. I asked her if they still have the crown. She said, laughing, it's called a tiara and she'd ask Pranav mama if he has it, when he comes home next. She also mentioned that Pranav mama wanted to be Miss World he was young and started giggling, just like Nilu. I don't understand girls, they giggle too much.

At dinner, I asked Mummy when Pranav mama would visit us next. He too lives in Delhi, though not with Nana and Nani. He visits us over the weekend when we are here. I had asked because I was bored, and everyone was too quiet. Nani was about to say something, but Nana butted in, 'He thinks my house is a hotel. He comes and goes whenever he pleases. But that is not how it works; you tell him that. I am done with that boy.' Nana says that often. He does not mean it. He only says that when he is tired and cannot think of anything else. He had said he was done with me as well when I did not do pranayam in the park with him that day. He doesn't mean it. Nana is usually less grumpy in the park, I have noticed. But then, at the dinner table, he was sulking. Nani told him to calm down, asking if had taken his pre-meal insulin injection. Snorting in reply, Nana continued eating. He has high blood sugar; I have heard everyone say; he has to take injections. His blood must be very sweet, like Rasna – no, no, like Roohafza!

I asked Mummy if she will ask Pranav mama to bring the tiara this time around. Frowning, she asked me to finish my *dal*. Nana snorted again. Maybe I should not have asked. Nani asked if I wanted more rice. She loves me the most.

I am not allowed to eat in the room. Nilu is. I always have to eat at the dining table. I don't even get a special plate. Nani gave a special plate to Nilu. She said Nilu can keep it for herself. She gets special treatment. Then Nana asked, 'Manu, are you excited to meet Papa tomorrow? Will you miss us when you go back?' I nodded my head. I asked if we could take Papa along on our morning walks and do pranayam. Nana started laughing and patted my back. His chin wobbles when he laughs.

My grandmother asked Mummy if the girl had eaten something. 'Very little,' she said. I asked her if Nilu would stay with us. Mummy said yes, she would. She even said she would need some counselling.

'From the counsellor? I asked.

'Yes … maybe.'

But I guess she was saying that to herself because she was looking at the room in which Nilu was sitting. I know about counsellors. There is one at my school. She gives away toffees when you meet her and smiles a lot. But you can't go to her just for toffees. You're sent to her if you do something naughty: if you don't complete your homework often or speak rudely to a teacher. I didn't know what Nilu had done, or why she needed a counsellor.

When I woke up, I found Papa next to me. I hugged him tightly in joy. He had come to take us back. He does that every year. Except the previous year when he could not come because … I don't remember the reason, but Mummy and I had travelled in a plane. Something rumbles in your tummy when the plane takes off. Mummy had thought I would be scared, or would vomit. But I am a brave boy; I was angry because I fell asleep, and Mumbai came too soon. I hate sleeping. Didn't I tell you everything happens very fast when I sleep?

Nani makes a lot of food when Papa comes. So many things. Both Nana and Nani smile a lot around him, like the school counsellor. They don't even scold me. Only Mummy scolds me and I run to Papa then. I told him about Nilu. He said Mummy had told him about her over the phone. I asked him if Nilu would come with us to Mumbai. 'We will see about that,' he said, kissing my head. 'Why don't you go and play with her for now?' Nani grinned at us.

I knew they wanted to talk about Nilu. But I didn't care. I had to watch *Chhota Bheem* on television. I went into the room where Nilu was folding the laundry; I asked her if she watched TV. She shook her head to say no. 'We don't have TV, baba,' she added. I asked how she watched cartoons then. She said she watched them at her neighbour's house sometimes. When I told her she could watch them with me now, she smiled – not her usual annoying giggle but an honest smile, the kind I have when Mummy says I can play another round of my favourite game on her phone. She said she had to first finish folding clothes. I can easily leave any work for television. Nilu is different. She either works or sleeps. On the train to Mumbai, she mostly slept. She didn't even eat the snacks they serve as soon as the train starts. I saved her two Eclairs toffees from my tray.

Since then, she lives with us. Today when I explained to Nilu what is April Fools' Day, she said she had never played an April Fools' prank before. She didn't even know the names of all the months when she first came to live with us. I had to teach her the names of the days of the week and the months of the year. She said she had once hidden her mother's purse in the sack of potatoes after which her mummy, who had been looking for it, started cursing everyone. I told her cursing was rude.

But I liked the idea. We decided to hide Papa's wallet along with his iPad and his mobile phone. He would think they were lost and search around the house; just when he gives up, we would scream, 'April Fool!'

Papa is bathing and Mummy is in the kitchen. Nilu says we should hide my father's things inside the drawer under my bed. She is stupid. Mummy can easily find it here. I have decided to hide these things in Sid's room, my classmate and best friend who lives across the road. Today is the last day of our break. From tomorrow, the new session starts. Sid and I are excited to go to the new class. I have a brand-new school bag too. The red one with Superman on it. Last night Mummy sat and covered all my new notebooks and labelled them. I asked her if Nilu will also come to my school with me. She didn't say anything and just exchanged looks with Papa. Then Papa said we should give Nilu time to get familiar with the area and the city before we start sending her to school with me.

I didn't get it. She already knows the area quite well – better than me. She keeps going out to get things. Mummy never lets me cross the road alone. She says the road is very busy. Busy road means risky, Papa told me. But Mummy also says the same thing about Papa – that he is always busy. But he doesn't look risky. I've come to know that you don't always get what your parents say; they seem to have a language of their own. And in that language, busy means risky.

But Mummy sends Nilu to Sid's house often to bring wheat grass juice that his mother makes every morning – it's yuck to taste though! That means Nilu knows how to cross the road. I am taking her along with me to Sid's place. I've put the iPad, wallet and phone in the new red school bag of mine. I've told Nilu to not make any noise while we sneak out, all she needs to do is to help me cross the road. She has just smiled and nodded. I guess that's a yes. She's a little funny that way, Nilu. But maybe I am starting to understand her ways now. If this April Fools' prank works, then I guess I can call her my next best friend after Sid.

Unruly Sun

'WHAT WAS THE name of the poet you had mentioned?' asked Samar, without looking at Angai. His gaze remained fixed on the road. The traffic was unusually light for a Monday morning.

'John Donne,' Angai replied absently, gazing out of the window. For the next few minutes that they were together, neither of them uttered a word. The silence between them stung Angai, but he couldn't think of anything to break it. The sight of the approaching metro station threw him into relief.

'Well ... here we are,' Samar said. 'Ping me when you get home, okay? All the best for the exam.'

'Sure. Thanks for the ride.' Angai wondered if pressing Samar's hand at this point would seem odd. They weren't friends or lovers. And they both knew it was unlikely they'd become either. Any strings of attachment had to be snipped, rolled up and swallowed, no matter if they choked on them.

On this cold yet sunny December morning, Angai watched Samar's car drive away from outside the metro station until it was indiscernible in the distance.

It hadn't been long since they'd started messaging each other on Planet Romeo, a dating website.

Angai had stumbled upon Samar's profile, 'Delhi_Guy'. It clearly looked experimental – made hastily and out of curiosity. It didn't care to impress. On the other hand, Angai's profile had been thoughtfully crafted – every word out of the 350 he'd used. He described himself as 'ample-bodied', instead of large. Every photograph had been carefully picked – left profiles only – with captions quoting Barthes, Foucault and Sontag.

Delhi_Guy had only one picture, showing the lower half of his face, while most of the remaining sections had been left blank. His bio read, *'Discreet, well-educated, well-travelled. A conversation to begin with? Exploring ...'*

Angai decided to skip ahead, but the website had registered his visit. Two days later, he found a message in his inbox: *'Hi, Went thru ur profile & found it vry intrstng n diffrnt. Was wondrng if u'd like to chat further?'*

It was the same half-faced man whose profile Angai had found too lazily written to warrant a response.

Later in the evening, on his way back home from work, he received another message: *'Hi, dnt gt me wrng bt I really found ur write-up intrstng. I hope u dnt think of me as a creepy stalker. M a civil engineer by profession. Wud u like 2 grab a cup of coffee sumtym?'*

Angai revisited the profile, looking for any redeeming features he might have missed the last time. It was still bare. He then thought of things Delhi_Guy could have written that would have irked him more. Maybe leaving things unsaid was a lesser crime than writing foolish things. He could have put up a picture of a celebrity captioned *'Not mine pic'* below it. Angai didn't have a long prescription for his prospective dates: be fit, tall, athletic, sane, sorted, decent, non-fat, non-girlish, non-uncle, non-*attitudey,* non-hairy, not out and loud, etc.

Delhi_Guy didn't seem to have these prejudices or knew better than to broadcast them. Or maybe he was just lazy to type them. Most importantly, he had refrained from using the clichéd yet accurate euphemism for casual sex one usually found on such sites: *looking for friends and fun.*

'Hi Delhi_Guy. I am Angai. How are you? Thanks for appreciating the write-up. I couldn't find much on your profile, though. Umm ... calling you Delhi_Guy sounds weird. May I know your name?'

Later that night, just as Angai had made himself comfortable in the bed, a message beeped on his phone. It was Delhi_Guy: *'Hi Angai. Datz an exotic name uv chosen 4 urself! But I hvnt thot of an alternate name & m not cmfr8bl revealing my real name yet. M new to dis "world". Bt maybe u cud call me Samar. I dint write a lot coz nobdy really cares 2 read. Wat do u do?'*

Angai frowned at his phone screen, reading the message twice. He felt too irritated to clarify it was not a pseudonym and too tired to explain why he found it pointless to fashion one. So, he put off responding until the next morning. But it marked the beginning of a conversation.

It had been a month since Samar had made a profile on Planet Romeo. *'A frnd told me abt it whn I went to the US dis summer. So I thot I'd see wats d fuss all abt. M just testing d waters. Trust us Indians 2 turn anything 2 trash. Lol!,'* he had said in one of the first few exchanges. His messages continued to make Angai frown as he read them but he responded nevertheless, even if to correct Samar's politics. Samar was never defensive, though. Either he did not mind being instructed or was too infatuated to let his ego be a barrier in this channel of communication. This ensured a steady flow of messages between the two; until one day, in one of the messages, Samar shared his mobile number, asking if Angai would want to talk over the phone or use WhatsApp to make the conversation more real time.

When there was no response from Angai for almost a week, Samar had begun to regret his foolhardiness. But then one night, while working on his laptop, he received a message. It was from Angai.

Hi, sorry for the delayed response. Me and my friends had been occupied with organizing a support group of queer kids who face violence at the hands of their family after coming out. We have been trying to put together a resource kit for such kids. It's heart-breaking to hear some of their stories.

Coming to your request about exchanging phone numbers ... I think it's best we restrict our conversations to PR for now. I think both of us are not really sure about each other. You don't trust me enough to share your real name with me, and I don't trust you enough to give my number. I think we are even, aren't we?

Frankly, I am past the days of excessive caution. I don't mind giving you my number, but you must promise that you will not misconstrue my lack of instantaneous replies as coldness or, worse still, impoliteness. After all, a phone number is no longer a door that can be knocked on politely. Especially due to WhatsApp, it has turned into an open window for everyone to barge in whenever they please.'

Later, Samar would make fun of this bloated idiom, lying naked beside him. 'I thought you were a pompous asshole! I thought to myself, *Why is he using words such as "promise"*,' he would go on to say in their intimate moments, making Angai laugh at himself.

At the time, however, Samar wrote an equally long message in reply.

'Angai, I understand your apprehension. I don't know how to prove my credibility. If it reassures you, I can share my real name and send you a picture of my passport too. Though you are past your days of caution, I am still new to this world. I don't know whom to trust and how much to reveal. Do you think I go around sharing my number with everyone here? I enjoyed talking to you. You're different from others here. Thus, I made the request. I leave it to you to make the final decision. Should you disapprove, I won't message you from here on. But if you share your number, I promise to never take undue advantage of it.'

Perhaps, it was the tone and style of the message that set things in motion. Angai smiled. The next message he sent was directly to Samar's phone.

Thus began the rounds of regular good night/good morning messages that were, more than anything else, excuses to initiate a conversation. More pictures were exchanged, and with that, nascent hopes were raised. Though there was nothing extraordinary about Samar's looks, he smiled candidly revealing his evenly shaped teeth in almost every picture.

A week later, when Angai was busy fretting over an adamant runtime error in his code, he saw Samar's name flash on his cell phone. Startled, he stared at the persistently vibrating phone. He wondered how to mask his nervousness.

He rehearsed the opening line in his head at least twice before answering: 'Hey, what a pleasant surprise! I wasn't expecting your call. How is it going?'

Despite the awkward pauses and overlaps, the conversation helped the both of them overcome their hesitation. Telephonic conversations made Angai restive. He would embark on his own train of thoughts triggered by something the other person said and thereby lose track of the subsequent chat. Thus, over the phone, he always sounded a little lost. However, he found Samar's voice calming. It reminded him of the large antique teakwood desk his grandfather had owned. Like the desk, Samar's voice was smooth, polished and quaint.

Over the next few days, their messages grew more graphic and conversations more honest. But Angai realized that they had very little in common apart from the irrational desire that consumed the both of them. Samar, a few years his senior, was not exclusively attracted to men. His queerness, Angai realized, was a mere footnote to his overall existence. Also, it was only recently that Samar had started to explore his bisexuality, whereas queerness, for Angai, was at the nucleus of his existence. There was so much in his life that was shaped by it and from it. On his Twitter bio, he called himself 'an IT professional by day and a gay rights activist by night'. He also ran a popular community blog called 'Queeriosity'.

Recently, a Supreme Court verdict reinstating homosexuality as an act against 'the order of nature' had left Angai fuming; from Samar, it could not elicit anything more than an 'Oh! That's sad. This country is in deep shit!' For Samar, bisexuality was like a dinner jacket he could don for an evening party and then, once done, put it back inside the closet where it belonged.

'Look, I will eventually get married and settle down. I want to have kids; I like them,' Samar had told him candidly.

The practical implications of such realizations were not lost on Angai; often, he went through them in his head while staring at Samar's display picture on WhatsApp, minutes after concluding their late-night conversations. Perhaps that was the reason he was avoiding meeting Samar in person.

On one Tuesday, Samar rang up to plan a meeting; Angai had been home, trying to read for an upcoming exam but mostly eating and stressing instead. Although it took some effort to persuade Angai, he agreed finally. And so, after nearly two months since their first exchange of messages, they decided to see each other at a coffee shop near Samar's workplace.

'Thanks for drawing me out. I think I needed this; I was feeling cooped up,' Angai said, plopping down on the couch.

'Well, it's a wonderful evening. It should not have gone to waste. I am glad you came,' Samar said. 'Turn around and look.'

Behind them was a glass wall overlooking the busy Barakhamba Road. Angai turned around. It was a pretty evening indeed, mellowed by the December chill, the streets outside illuminated by the yellow light of street lamps.

At this point there was hardly anything new to be discovered that either of them would have wanted to reveal. However, they stole glances at each other. With all the pictures and messages they had exchanged over the past two months, each of them had outlined a mental portrait of the other. Now, in each other's presence, they could redraw a few curves, soften a few edges, accentuate others, and re-fill the gaps that until now were overflowing with colours of imagination.

A slick-haired, bespectacled, thirty-something man in a suit had appeared in front of Angai. He looked perfect to be a manager, Angai thought. But despite his manager-like appearance, Samar didn't have an overbearing personality. His speech was peppered with local phrases that exuded a strong Delhi influence. On the other hand, Samar found the deep purple scarf around Angai's neck too loud for his taste but could not deny that it went well with his radiant complexion.

'You know, you look Bong – studious and sincere – but you speak like a true Delhi*wallah*,' Angai commented while stirring sugar in his coffee.

'I have lived here all my life. Nowadays, I am just reminded of my Bengaliness during Durga Pujo and weddings,' Samar said. He took a spoonful of his banoffee pie and raised it to Angai's mouth. After some seconds of hesitation, Angai took the bite.

'I am not going to share my brownie, you know,' he said, wiping the cream from his lips.

'So you think.' Samar smiled warmly.

They spoke on a variety of subjects. There was a nervous undercurrent to Angai's speech, Samar could sense. He spoke with an urgency of someone who was afraid of his thoughts slipping away if not pinned immediately with words. But he spoke effusively about his blog; he believed it helped raise voices of people from the community. Samar also observed the slight change in Angai's timbre at the word 'community' as if it were a private, intimate matter to which Samar was an outsider.

'Do you write every day?' Samar asked.

'Not every day. I work at a full-time job, so it's difficult to find the time. Two of my friends help run the blog. But I write whenever I feel impelled to. Last night, I wrote about gay men not having to fear embracing their effeminacy,' Angai said. A light flashed on his phone. Curbing the urge to check the notifications, he continued, 'In fact, we are planning to curate more content from the community. More guest posts and suchlike.'

'How do you think one should embrace their effeminacy?' Samar asked, half frowning.

'In many ways. With something as trivial as – I don't know – donning this scarf or wearing kohl, maybe.'

'Wear it the next time then,' Samar said, leaning back into the couch. 'As for the scarf, I really like it.'

Angai was rather dubious if Samar truly meant that. Nevertheless, they chatted until they were the only ones left in the upper storey of the coffee shop.

As they walked towards the metro station, hand in hand, Samar planted a light kiss on Angai's cheek.

'Your hands are damp,' Samar said.

'It happens when I am nervous,' Angai blurted, suddenly conscious of his damp hands.

The alley was deserted by now. The cold air made Angai want to go back inside the cafe and order another cup of hot coffee.

'Can I kiss you?' Samar asked as they walked on. Angai nodded.

'I should've kissed you in the cafe. We were alone there,' Samar said.

'Better late than never, I guess,' Angai laughed. How desperate he must have sounded, he thought the next second. They kissed once before Angai slipped inside the metro station.

Later that night, browsing through his Twitter feed, Angai was occupied with thoughts about Samar. Never had his feelings been so ambivalent. For once, he wished his feelings could be insulated from his politics. Why should it matter that Samar was not as outraged by the Supreme Court judgment and chose to go out for drinks with his friends rather than join the protest at the Jantar Mantar ground along with Angai? Why should it matter that Samar would choose the convenient path by marrying a woman and having babies? Why must the impermanence of their bond prevent him from enjoying it while it lasted? Was there even a bond to begin with? He wished he could enjoy the present without having to dissect his feelings.

There are days
when the toughest battle
I fight with myself
is to not to love you silly.
And then falls night,
dressing my wounds
with its darkness,
dunking me in
the relief and relish
of loss!

Less than a week later, Samar convinced his parents to take a short trip so that he could have the house to himself and Angai could be invited to stay with him.

'But I have to study for an exam. I cannot spare more than a night,' Angai said over the phone when Samar revealed the plan to him.

'Don't be difficult. Bring your books, you can study here.'

'Um ... are you sure about this?'

'Listen, I've had to pull a lot of strings to make this work. You have to come, alright, even if for a night?'

The strings had begun to sprout.

When Angai reached, Samar asked him to come directly into the bedroom to 'hang out' for a bit. Above the bed, there were pictures of Samar performing on stage.

'Is that really you?'

'Yes, I dabbled in theatre in college. I was told I was quite good.'

'I can barely recognize you.

'Yeah, well!'

They were lying in bed next to each other watching TV when Samar said, 'I am a bad kisser. But I'd like to kiss you.' Angai consented, feeling glad that Samar had taken the lead.

Off came the clothes one by one. They rolled on the carpeted floor in each other's embrace, kissing and then kissing some more. For minutes their gaze remained locked as they lay, taking turns, on top of each other, studying each other's faces up close.

'Samar, it's starting to hurt,' Angai said, nudging Samar's face away.

'Don't be a wuss! It's a love bite. It looks pretty, see!' he said and gently kissed the red splotch on Angai's fair neck. 'And why are you still calling me 'Samar'? You know my real name now.'

'Because I prefer 'Samar'. Dare you use it again with anyone else. It's mine now,' he said, lifting his head to bite Samar's shoulder. 'Only mine.'

Samar's moves convinced Angai he hadn't been with too many men in the past. Yet so fulfilling was this intimacy that they both climaxed together.

They lay on the carpet afterwards, spent, their limbs entangled, when Samar whispered, 'Listen—' He propped his head on his hand and blew over Angai's face, 'Can we take a break?'

Angai traced Samar's collar bone with his thumb. As his other hand travelled south, he discovered Samar was flaccid.

'There's a report I need to finalize,' Samar said, sitting up, his voice tender with exhaustion and affection. 'I have a meeting early tomorrow morning.'

While Samar was punching keys on his laptop and he was perusing his notes, Angai saw what he had always envisioned in his head, even if for that one night. The sense of security; the loving presence of a man in the background as he continued working; the luxury of having someone to make love to, someone to tease and crack jokes with, when the tedium of life and its chores took over. This was what Angai had always longed for. He went on reading his notes and, for a moment, he felt his body hum with contentment.

Samar got up and walked to the kitchen, followed by the clinking sound of dishes and water streaming from a tap. He returned with butter-and-jam toasts and two glasses filled with Sprite and ice.

'This is all I could manage,' he said, setting the tray in front of Angai. 'I have some fine vodka to go with this if you would like a drink.'

'You didn't have to do this. I wasn't particularly hungry anyway,' Angai said.

'Why don't you just shut up and eat? Do not tell me you are on a diet. We have a few eggs; if you want, I can fix you an omelette.'

'No, thanks,' Angai said. 'But vodka would be great.'

'See, now you're talking,' replied Samar, rising to fetch the bottle from his cabinet.

He was treating Angai with a sense of irreverence, which Angai realized, was Samar's attempt to establish a bond, his way of showing affection. In this middle-class, domestic setting, dressed in track pants as he mocked Angai playfully, Samar was removed from his managerial aura and had become even more accessible and endearing.

By the time Samar climbed back into the bed, it was late. Angai had dozed off, curled up with his notes close to his chest, lips slightly parted. Samar covered him with the quilt and hugged him. Angai opened his eyes and smiled. 'Done, are we?'

Samar sealed Angai's mouth with a kiss. They were locked in an embrace now, his breath warm on Angai's neck. 'I like you. I really like you. I find you very attractive. I like you as a guy … without the kohl,' Samar said.

'But that is an integral part of me, Samar. I can't deny myself that,' Angai said, his hands cupping Samar's face.

'Hmm.' Samar nuzzled into his neck. Running fingers through Samar's hair, Angai knew Samar was not fully convinced.

'You don't need to worry,' Angai said, his fingers grazing Samar's face. 'You won't have to put up with it. Soon you will find someone sanctioned by society who can have your babies too.'

At the crack of dawn, Angai felt Samar's hands working up his body. He hugged Angai from behind as he nibbled on his earlobe. They wanted to fuck again, but the ticking clock was a brutal reminder of the reality that awaited them outside the warmth of their quilt. Samar peered at the clock. It was half-past six.

'I don't want you to get late for work, sir. It's time to get your ass off the bed.'

'I still have half an hour at hand,' Samar pleaded.

'You know, this reminds me of a poem by John Donne about two lovers who chide the sun for intruding into their chamber and announcing their separation,' Angai said.

Samar bathed him in a desirous glance. 'You're such a nerd.'

'Must you go? Can't you call in sick?' Angai asked.

'I wish I could. I have a really important meeting today –

you know the one I was preparing for last night,' Samar said, burrowing his face in Angai's neck. 'Who'd want to leave this warm bed and you otherwise?'

'Go, get ready,' said Angai.

Samar left the bed. Angai watched him keenly – still cocooned in the quilt and despair – for a few minutes before falling asleep again. The sun was finally up.

When this dream ends
like all others do,
all I wish to take with me is
a shirt that smells of you

'Would you like some milk in your tea?' Samar asked, ruffling Angai's hair, who struggled to open his eyes.

'I'll make it.'

'I have made tea already. Just answer milk or not.'

'I'll have it with milk, thank you.'

Angai was warned before he took the first sip. 'The tea is shitty.'

He had resolved to be lenient since he knew Samar was not comfortable with cooking, but the tea tasted so poor, it crushed his willpower and he muttered: 'Shitty, indeed.' Samar looked at him innocently.

'I'll make it afresh. You carry on,' Angai said. He was making tea in Samar's kitchen. He had never done this before. He had never made tea in the morning for any of his dates. Neither had anyone made love to him first thing in the morning when he was raw and unprepared.

Soaking in the newness of this experience, Angai sat at the table, sipping tea, as Samar scampered along the length of the house looking for his things. It all seemed so natural to him. For a moment, Angai imagined himself a part of this household. It seemed like a daily affair, which would repeat the next day, as it had happened today.

To his dismay, though, his tea did not turn out to be any better. They would both laugh about it in the car later.

'I will drop you at Indraprastha metro station; it's on my way,' said Samar. They hugged, holding on to each other a moment too long before exiting.

It was a pleasant winter morning. The sun shone brightly. In the car, good music played on the radio.

'It was the milk that had gone bad,' said Angai, rolling down the window.

'Yeah, right! Blame the milk,' Samar sniggered and put on his sunglasses. 'Do you usually make tea for your dates?'

'No, I don't. But do not read too much into it,' Angai said sharply, snipping the strings before they could form knots.

'By the way, I read your blog the other day. I think you write well.'

'What did you read? The poem?'

'Yes, very impressive. The metaphors were quite fresh.'

Angai gave Samar a look. 'What do you know about metaphors and poetry?'

'More than you, dodo.'

With every passing moment, the dreamy landscape coloured with memories of the previous night was receding further into the background, as the starkness of reality edged itself firmly between the two of them. The closer they moved to the destination, the graver their tones and greyer the subjects of conversation.

'So, will you settle down with someone eventually, Angai?'

'Of course, I would like to,' Angai said. He was scrolling down his phone screen with his thumb. 'That is if we are not deemed criminals by the law.'

'Still stuck on that, are we?'

'I can't afford not to. I am gay, you see,' Angai said in an almost accusatory tone. Samar changed the song on the radio.

'What about you?' The question carried the same sourness that made Samar a bit uncomfortable.

'Well, almost everyone my age in my family is married now.' To lighten the mood, he added, 'Mother says she thought it was difficult to find matches for girls.'

'I am sure it's just a matter of time,' Angai said.

'If only you were not a man,' Samar said under his breath, not looking at Angai directly.

'Why did you just say that?'

'I didn't say *anything*!'

'Oh, come on!'

'I was just quoting Frederick, the seventeenth-century Prussian king.'

'I don't remember Frederick saying any such thing.'

'Of course he said it.'

'For whom?'

'For Voltaire, the French philosopher, his friend and his ...' He looked at Angai and winked.

'What nonsense! Do you mean Frederick and Voltaire were an item?'

'Well, do you know what Voltaire said of Frederick?'

'No, do you?'

'Do you want me to quote him?'

'If you can.'

'Perhaps you don't know,' Samar said, taking off his sunglasses, 'but when Voltaire had moved to Prussia, he was assigned a "special suite" in the palace of Frederick. In one of his letters, Voltaire said that in Frederick, he had found the protection of a king, conversations of a philosopher and the charms of an agreeable man.'

'That doesn't prove anything,' Angai said, trying to provoke him further.

'Really? Then you should listen to what Frederick wrote to Voltaire in a letter.'

'Go on. I am all ears,' Angai said.

When the car halted at a traffic intersection, Samar reached for his bag kept on the rear seat and brought out his Kindle.

'Let me read to you what Frederick said to Voltaire.'

After making a few taps and swipes on the screen, he cleared his throat and started reading:

> You have done me great wrongs. I have forgiven them all, and I even wish to forget them. But if you had not to do with a madman in love with your noble genius, you would not have gotten off so well. Do you want to hear sweet things? Very well, I will tell you some truths. I esteem in you the finest genius that the ages have borne; I admire your poetry and I love your prose. Never has an author had a tact so keen, a taste so sure and delicate. You are charming

> in conversation; you know how to amuse and instruct at the same time. You are the most seductive being I know, capable of making yourself loved by all the world when you choose. You have such graces of mind that you can offend and yet at the same time deserve the indulgence of those who know you. In short, you would be perfect if you were not a man.

Angai looked at Samar in disbelief as Samar put back the gadget in his bag. The traffic began moving.

'In short, you would be perfect if you were not a man,' Samar said, pinching Angai's cheek before pulling the gear. 'You see, I was just quoting Frederick. And you thought only you could quote grand old white men, eh?'

Angai squinted as a glare of sunlight flashed into his eyes. He had never hated the sun more.

'Who was the poet you'd mentioned?'

'John Donne,' Angai replied absently, looking out of the window.

Busy old fool, unruly sun,
Why dost thou thus,
Through windows, and through curtains call on us?
Must to thy motions lovers' seasons run?

The Debate

ON THEIR FIRST day of college, Pranav Bhalla was sitting in the last row of the lecture hall when Rishabh Malwa met him. Rishabh walked up to the last row and sat beside Pranav. Pranav returned his 'hi' with a smile. They chatted for some time until the professor entered and lectured the class on taking the engineering course seriously and how life-altering the next four years would be for them.

After the class, Rishabh asked Pranav if he'd like to come to the canteen for a quick bite. Pranav shrugged. 'Dude, are you scared of the seniors? Or of being ragged?' Rishabh asked. When Pranav didn't say anything, Rishabh put his arm around Pranav's neck and squeezed it gently. 'Don't worry. When you're with me, nobody can dare to bother you. From now on, you're my bro. Just stick with me, okay?' he said. Pranav knew Rishabh was just as nervous, but he found the feigned confidence amusing, if not reassuring.

However, Rishabh was not able to play the knight in shining armour. The campus culture had changed a lot. Save a couple of odd cases reported in the hostel, there were no horrid instances of ragging. But their shared fondness for A. R. Rahman's music, dislike for mathematics and the professor and mutual affection for each other cemented their friendship.

By the end of their first year, Kalla (Namit Kalra), Malla (Rishabh Malwa) and Bhalla (Pranav Bhalla) had formed a squad. All three of them were from Delhi. Rishabh was decidedly the best looking out of the three and thus quite popular among girls. Namit was too absorbed in his books to find time for female attention, and Pranav did not care for any. It was not a surprise, then, when Rishabh started dating Anjana, a plain-looking girl from the electronics and communications department. Many of their batchmates, including Namit, wondered why Rishabh fell for her when he could have chosen anyone he wanted. They mocked him for it quite openly. But Pranav dismissed their comments, saying, 'Grow up, dude! Your thinking is so parochial. Anjana is different; she is ambitious and has a vision. What if she is not svelte? They like each other, and that's what matters.'

'Exactly!' Rishabh would defend his girlfriend. 'She is my kinda girl. I would choose brains over beauty any day.'

It was perhaps due to the confidence with which Pranav spoke – the evidence of his convent school education amply displayed in his usage of words like 'parochial' and 'svelte' – that had drawn Rishabh to him. Both had grown close as friends, significantly after Pranav had helped him pass the Physics exam by tutoring him for a whole night. It was difficult to tell whether it was only gratitude that drove Rishabh to plant a kiss on Pranav's cheek in front of everyone when the results were announced. Anyone could see how distracted Rishabh would get whenever Pranav skipped college. Rishabh was never at his best when Pranav was not around: He would laugh tepidly, look at his watch constantly or fidget with his cell phone, waiting for a text message from Pranav. Thanks to a special recharge, he was now able to send 1,000 free text messages every month to any five numbers. He chose Pranav, Namit, Anjana and his parents.

Pranav's indifference to dating, or girls in general, was something neither of his closest friends discussed with him. Instead, they attributed it to his generally private and shy demeanour.

But Rishabh had noticed how Pranav's neck craned from the back seat whenever their dashing fourth-year senior, Hamid, entered the bus. Though he never said anything, Rishabh would try to distract Pranav whenever Hamid was around. Driven partly by Hamid's charm and partly by curiosity to see Rishabh's reaction, Pranav started talking to Hamid on the pretext of gathering insights into the upcoming placement drives. Rishabh would listen to all the information Pranav passed on to him and Namit dolloped with lavish praise for the very helpful (and gorgeous) Hamid sir. 'Okay, can we go and get something to eat now?' he would say, standing up hastily, as if to shake off the praise for Hamid.

In their third year, Namit proposed a plan. Since both of his roommates were moving out, he asked Rishabh and Pranav to move in with him.

'It'll be great, Malla! Both the seniors are gone, so we can have the whole flat to ourselves. The best part is the landlord doesn't live here. He only comes once in two months to check on the house. The rent is reasonable as well. How does it sound?' Namit asked.

Rishabh loved the idea. Fed up with his meddlesome roommate, he was looking for another place anyway. He tried to convince Pranav of the idea. This way they could study together and access Kalla's legendary notes. Plus, the flat was closer to Anjana's PG accommodation.

'You think I should leave my room so you have easier access to your girlfriend and Kalla's notes?' Pranav enquired. 'You must be crazy.'

'Bhalla, don't act arrogant, *bhenchod*!' Namit said. Rishabh, who had already called Pranav's bluff, smiled. Within a week, the three also became flatmates.

With the newfound proximity of living together, Pranav couldn't help but notice Rishabh at ease: his full chest during his daily round of push-ups in the morning, his strong jawline when he shaved his face; or how he covered his face with his right arm while sleeping, revealing his mildly hairy armpit.

Moreover, Pranav observed how tactfully Rishabh handled the landlord on the issue of a rent hike; how easily he fixed the faulty room cooler; the way he took care of his girlfriend when her father died of lung cancer ('It's the cigarettes, Rishu, it's the cigarettes. I told him to quit smoking; he just wouldn't listen! You will have to quit smoking if you want us to go on ...' she had cried miserably in Rishabh's arms right before Pranav); the way he scored top marks in the exams with minimum hours of studying. Perhaps, some credit for those marks should have gone to Kalla for preparing the most comprehensive yet concise notes. But Namit was almost incidental to their experience of living together. He would spend most of his time in the library or the cyber cafe during the semester and would return to Faridabad, his hometown, as soon as the semester ended. Mostly, Rishabh and Pranav ended up being left behind.

When the intra-college debate competition was announced, Rishabh found himself in a fix. His girlfriend and his best friend were on opposing teams in the debate. Pranav was representing the department of computer science, and Anjana the department of electronics and communication.

'But isn't the matter in the court now? Isn't the case pending in the High Court? What's the point of debating it? The court will do what it has to,' Rishabh said to Anjana. He was hanging a bedsheet to dry on the clothesline. Next to his feet was a bucket filled with freshly washed clothes. It was late in the evening, and they were on the terrace of his flat. Anjana was sitting on the parapet, a few steps away from him. The twittering of mynas was overpowering the honking of the cars passing by at a distance.

'What do you mean? The matter is in the court – that is the whole point. How can the sexual lives of consenting adults be up for debate in the court of law? Don't you realize the absurdity of the whole thing, Rishu? It's ridiculous that we are even debating these matters in 2008. But we can and we must.' She skipped down from the parapet and walked towards him. From her impassioned speech, Rishabh felt sure she would emerge victorious in the debate. She leaned close and kissed him.

'How was it?' she asked.

He looked stunned. 'It was ... great ... amazing.'

'I know. And I won't listen to any damn court which says this kiss was illegal or wrong. Courts shouldn't get to decide whom we can sleep with or whom to love. We should,' she said and walked back to the parapet.

'Look, we are also consenting adults, and we are not even homosexuals; there's no one in the house right now. Nothing we do will be considered illegal, just so you know.' He winked at her as he wrung out water from a shirt.

Anjana shifted a little to perch herself properly on the parapet before continuing, 'Don't get carried away. I am not ready yet. I was simply making a point. How can you even think of such a thing right now?'

'Babe, I was teasing you. Even I am occupied with the placements right now. I have been appointed the placement coordinator, don't you know? And Satyam Infotech is visiting tomorrow,' he said.

'Do you think I should sit for Satyam too? Hardly any companies are visiting our branch, anyway,' she asked.

'Why not?' Rishabh's eyes lit up. 'Imagine Malla, Kalla, you and me working at the same organization. It will be great!'

'You're not helping, Rishu.'

'Don't you like my friends?'

Anjana silently gazed at the horizon. Jaipur's skyline was populated by the newly emerging malls, the medieval mahals, and the Aravalli hills. Far away, the sky began to crowd with large puffs of grey clouds which looked as though they had just been exhaled out of a colossal, sooty chimney.

'Anju, you did not answer. Which one of my friends do you not like?'

'It looks like it might rain. I think you should bring down the clothes,' Anajana said. 'I will iron your shirt for tomorrow's interview.'

Rishabh's interview did not go as planned. Just minutes before the final round, he had felt the urge to take a piss. After relieving his bladder, he proceeded to wash his hands. He forgot that the first tap of the ground floor lávatory had a faulty valve that lets out a violent jet of water as soon as it is opened. By the time he screwed the tap shut, his crisply ironed shirt was sprayed with water. He didn't even have time to exchange his shirt with a classmate. It was his turn to go in. He sat smiling before his interviewer, wearing a wet shirt and an air of dry confidence.

The results would be declared in after a week, the training and placement officer of their college had announced. Now, the only thing that preoccupied him was the upcoming debate competition.

Over the next two days, Rishabh helped Anjana rehearse her speech and made a few suggestions too. ('Here you need to sound a bit more assertive, Anju. Doesn't that sound kinda sentimental, baby? Could you revise it? Ah! Now that's a brilliant point.') But he had no clue what Pranav, who hadn't returned home for two days, had been up to.

The following day, when Rishabh asked him about his preparation in the college canteen, Pranav replied, 'Oh, it's great. Hamid sir let me use his laptop and the internet. Be prepared to console your girlfriend. She is going to lose this one.'

'Thank god, I am not one of the judges,' Rishabh said.

'You know, Malla, there are times in life when you must choose a side.'

Rishabh felt as though the words passing from Pranav's lips were not his own. But how tender those lips looked! He observed them for few seconds before saying, 'And don't you think you've chosen the wrong side?'

'What? What is the wrong side?'

'I mean *you* of all people should have argued in favour of the motion.'

As soon as he said it, Rishabh knew his choice of words had been wrong, but he did not flinch. Clearing his throat, he straightened his back as if preparing for a round of impromptu debate.

'Whatever the fuck is that supposed to mean? What are you trying to say, Malla?'

Rishabh looked at the fleet of buses standing outside the college gate. The first two had started moving. He knew this conversation was not unfolding as he had planned it in his head. He knew there was no way this conversation could conclude without his saying something that could hurt Pranav.

'Look, let's talk about this at the flat. The buses are moving. I have to borrow the lab file from Vikram. Then I have to submit mine tomorrow. I cannot miss the bus,' Rishabh said, standing up. 'Let's go. Vikram is in there too.' He slung his bag across his shoulder and picked up Pranav's bag too.

Pranav started typing an SMS on his phone. 'You go. I'll come later. Hamid sir is taking me on his bike. I will stay at his place for some time. I need to read a few articles on the internet,' he said, without looking at Rishabh.

'Are you sure? You could use the cybercafe in the next lane, you know. You've hardly been around for the last three days,' Rishabh said, sliding his hand into his pocket.

'Is that a problem too? Should I 'of all people' not go where I want to go? *Tu hai kaun, yaar*? *Baap hai kya mera*? Who the hell has appointed you as my chaperone? I will come home when I want to. You go, now. The buses are leaving.'

'You know what? You're just being an asshole for no reason. Fuck you, Bhalla!' He slammed Pranav's bag on the table.

Rishabh walked away from Pranav as fast as he could, away from how Pranav made him feel: affectionate, protective, possessive, angry and something else he could not quite name. 'Fuck you, Bhalla. Just fuck you! Damnit!' he muttered.

On the day of the debate, Rishabh woke up early and took a long shower. After making Maggi for himself, he woke up Pranav: '*Oye*, Bhalla! Get up and rehearse your speech. Get up, you bugger! Eat something, you'll need it.'

When Pranav grumbled about the shirts he had, Rishabh lent him one of his own. He then called up Anjana to check on how she was doing.

'Hey, angel! Morning. Are you ready, baby? ... Of course, I am going to reach there before you. I will be there in twenty minutes. I will meet you in the auditorium ... yes, he is ready too ... he is eating breakfast. Have you had yours? ... Sure, I will. Bye. Love you!'

Pranav was listening to the conversation, eating quietly. 'Is she ready?' he asked once Rishabh cut the call.

'Yeah, she says hi and wishes you luck.'

'Yeah … thanks,' Pranav said, forking the last bits of noodles left in his bowl. Though Pranav kept a straight face, Rishabh could sense the hint of a smile around his lips (oh, the tender lips!). He imagined Pranav setting down the bowl with a smile on his radiant face, as he looked Rishabh straight in his eyes and said, 'I am telling you, Malla, you will have to console your girlfriend. She is so losing this one.' He felt like knocking off the smug expression on Pranav's face with a punch. An image of Pranav's bruised face sprang up in his mind. He went to his room to put on his watch.

Of late, he had been fighting this intense feeling at regular intervals. The urge to punch his friend's face. He had felt it earlier this morning too, when Pranav was sleeping guilelessly with a pillow tucked under his left arm, only half of his lightly stubbled face visible. The image of Pranav's bruised face disgusted him. It wasn't so much this image, Rishabh realized, as he searched for his watch in the drawer that made him uneasy; it was the urge to touch Pranav's face that disgusted him. 'Bhalla, have you seen my watch?' he yelled. 'I think I lent it to you.'

'No idea … ask Namit!' replied Pranav. 'Malla, I feel like having a beer.'

He found the watch beneath his tutorial sheets, hiding, like Pranav's smug smile.

'Did you hear me? I feel like having a beer!' Pranav called out again.

'*Abey maar khayega kya, chutiye?*' Rishabh yelled, as he fastened the watch strap on his wrist. This boy was impossible!

But when he came out dressed and ready to leave and saw

Pranav smiling brightly, he said: 'You know what, let's get beer tonight to celebrate—'

'What? Her victory or mine?' Pranav cut him short.

Rishabh cursed himself for walking into this trap; he knew no reply would sound sincere and convincing. Nevertheless, he said, 'Neither. To celebrate our last semester together.' He saw Namit walking into the living room, rubbing his eyes.

'Hey, do we have something to eat? I am starving,' Namit said. He was wearing shorts and a vest, a size too short for him, or maybe he had gained some weight again.

Rishabh said happily, 'No, I made Maggi for Bhalla, because he is the debate boy today. But there's some bread in the fridge and two eggs, too.'

Namit smiled faintly. He was still drowsy. 'All the best, Bhalla!' He then turned towards Rishabh and asked, 'Malla, do you have a cigarette?'

'Are you still sleepy, dude? You know that I've stopped smoking since Anjana's father's death'

'You're such a wuss! Why did you stop smoking because her father died?

'She is sensitive about this issue. You won't get it. You haven't lost someone so close to you from an illness.'

'Now don't lecture me right in the morning. Ask Chottu to get me a pack when you see him downstairs,' Namit said, scratching his belly. '*Achha*, I am going home today.' He yawned.

'You won't stay for the debate?' Rishabh asked

Namit shook his head as he opened the fridge. 'Ma has organized a special pooja so that I get a job before the semester ends. She is tired of fielding questions from our relatives now.

But I will be back soon.' Taking out all the remaining slices of bread, he exclaimed, 'Dude, there's only four left!'

Pranav stepped out of his room, holding Rishabh's and his bag. 'The bus is almost here. Let's go,' he said.

'All the best, Bhalla! Also ... don't forget to send Chhotu with my cigarettes ...' Namit yelled as they descended the stairs.

They reached the venue on time. After wishing luck to Pranav and Anjana, Rishabh sat in the last row of the auditorium. 'You look more nervous than the participants,' a classmate sitting next to him joked. 'Relax!'

Later that night, after what felt like a long time, Rishabh felt extremely anxious and homesick. He paced up and down the room, with headphones on, switching between different FM channels on his cell phone. Anjana had not responded to any of his calls and messages. For a moment, he considered going over to her flat, even though she had repeatedly told him not to since the landlady knew her parents. The next moment, imagining her even more furious, he dropped the idea and dialled her number again. The mechanical voice blared: *'The number you're trying to reach is either currently switched off or out of service area.'*

He wrote another text message: *Babe it ws jst a db8. Dnt tk it so personally. Plz call me! M worried!! Plzzz!*

At the sound of a bike halting outside, he stepped onto the balcony. In the dim glow of the street lamp, Rishabh saw Pranav holding something solid in one hand as he shook hands with Hamid.

It was a small crate of beer, Rishabh noticed when he opened the door.

'Malla, you wanted to celebrate, right? Let's celebrate tonight!' Pranav said, raising the crate high in the air.

'Thanks ... but I don't feel like having a beer right now,' Rishabh replied coolly and went back to the balcony. Setting the crate on the table, Pranav poured himself a glass of water; he wasn't sure whether he was thirsty or worried. This was not how Rishabh usually responded to an offer of beer. Something was immensely wrong. Had he taken the game too far? Had he actually hurt Malla? He walked over to the balcony.

Rishabh was smoking. 'Bhalla, congratulations once again, *yaar*,' he said softly as Pranav stood beside him.

'Thank you,' Pranav said. 'Dude ... have you started smoking again?'

'Yes ... felt like a smoke. It's not a big deal.'

'Look, Rishabh, I am sorry, okay? One of us had to win. It could have been her too. It's not my fault really that I won. I feel bad about her. About you ... I feel awful,' Pranav said, resting his arm on Rishabh's shoulder. There was silence for a few minutes. Because Rishabh was taller, Pranav had to stretch his arm clumsily. He visualized them standing on the balcony like this. The scene must have looked awkward.

'Malla, drop that cigarette and say something. You know Anjana will lose her mind if she finds out you're smoking.' Pranav attempted to wiggle out of this posture and the heavy silence. 'Did you talk to her? How is she?'

'Yeah, I just got off the phone with her. She will be fine, you know. It's just a debate, I told her,' Rishabh replied. He looked unusually calm. 'I feel tired. I think I'll crash.'

'Sure,' said Pranav, putting the crate of beer inside the refrigerator.

The crate of beers was brought out the next week. They were celebrating: the results of the campus placement drive were out, and to his surprise, Rishabh had received a job offer from Satyam Infotech. He was initially disappointed that Pranav did not make the cut and thought it might be inappropriate to celebrate, but as the night advanced, the froth of the beer washed away his scruples. Rishabh was taking large swigs of beer, laughing heartily as he mimicked their first-year English professor. Pranav had thought the beer would help him forget his own disappointment so he could partake in Rishabh's joy. He was sitting on the bed, while Rishabh, dressed in his faded blue T-shirt and boxers, sat cross-legged on the floor. The marble floor felt cool under his bare, long legs.

Rishabh carefully placed his bottle on the floor. He then stood up and spoke with exaggerated flourish: 'I am tired of teaching you Palestines. You have no value for literary art. You thrive on the monks and their Ferraris and these new-fangled Five Pointers, even though it is complete garbage! You so-called future technocrats,' he raised his hands at this point and made air quotes before picking up the bottle of beer, 'I am done with you uncouth people.'

'Malla, this is your last beer. You're so drunk.'

'I am not drunk, you *jaaackass*. Why do you say that?'

'It's *philistines,* not Palestines,' Pranav said, trying hard to reel in his laughter.

'Oh, fuck! Philistines ... yes ... that's what I meant!' He leaned on the wall and laughed, his back pressed hard against the wall.

'What was with all the air quotes she made?' Pranav said, taking a sip from his bottle.

'I know, right? At first I didn't understand why she keeps making strange gestures all the time.' He laughed some more as he wobbled towards the bed.

They were enveloped in silence now – Rishabh was reminded of the times in college when they sat discussing, or mostly dissing, a teacher on the lawns, as the same teacher would suddenly pass them by. He sat next to Pranav on the bed and said: 'I miss those days, Bhalla. Our first year was wonderful.'

'You miss it?'

'Yes, don't you? We had great teachers. We were all so naïve. The first time we met, we were in the same class. Then you and Kalla chose the computer science department while I was stuck in the information technology department. Things changed after the first year.'

'Then you fell in love with Anjana in our second year,' Pranav said, staring into blank space. 'You're right – things changed.'

There was again a short, stinging spell of silence. Rishabh turned to face Pranav directly with a strange look on his face. 'Hey, your Hamid sir,' he said. 'Why is he still in Jaipur? Shouldn't be off to Bangalore or Mysore or someplace else?'

'No, he plans to expand his father's business. He says he doesn't want to be just an employee. He may do an MBA, though; he is such a cool guy ...'

'I see.' Rishabh popped two salted peanuts in his mouth, one after another. 'You have really grown close, haven't you? Like, very chummy.'

'He is a senior. I look up to him, and he is fond of me. That's it.' Pranav's hands were sweaty. He tightened his grip on the bottle and nervously drank from it.

'Please drop the act, Bhalla! Don't act so naïve, at least not in front of me.' Rishabh's voice was firm. 'How many times have you guys fucked?' he asked with a straight face.

'Have you lost your mind, Malla? What are you implying?'

'Why does this question bother you? I am just asking how many times has Hamid fucked you? It's a simple question, Pranav Bhalla.'

Pranav shuffled to get up. His mouth had gone dry. This was not the Rishabh he had known.

Rishabh held Pranav's hand. 'Did he fuck you well? Did you take his cock deep in your ass?' With a jerk, Rishabh pushed Pranav back. Losing his balance, Pranav flopped down onto the bed.

'Malla, you're out of your senses. I don't want to talk to you right now. Just let me go!'

'Go where? To Hamid? *Haan …? Saaley gaandu*! You bloody homo!'

These words issued from Rishabh's mouth much like the violent jet of water from that faulty tap from their college lavatory, soaking his shirt in bitterness that felt oddly cathartic. And again he felt a queer mix of audacity and embarrassment.

While he kept a straight, unfazed face, inside he was crumbling.

But those two words sent blood pounding in Pranav's veins. He collected himself, and descended on Rishabh with all the force he could muster. He looked Rishabh straight in the eyes and struck him. He was prepared to duck to defend himself, but when Rishabh did not retaliate, Pranav slapped him hard once again. 'You motherfucking bastard! How dare you? I will shred you to pieces if you ever utter those words again. I will fuck you up, Rishabh Malwa. I will tear you apart.'

Rishabh stared at Pranav in astonishment. His face was singeing from the blow of Pranav's slap and his hands were pinned down. Pranav was sitting astride his chest as though possessed, his face aflame with anger and jaws clenched.

'Do you love him?' Rishabh asked, his voice drained of the aggression as he choked with emotion.

Digging his thumbnails into Rishabh's wrists, Pranav collapsed on his chest. If it were not for the loud and steady rumble of the big metallic room cooler, Pranav's groan would have alarmed the next-door neighbours. His body was trembling with rage.

Rishabh rubbed Pranav's back affectionately, waiting for his breathing to become normal. 'It's okay, bro. You're safe,' he whispered, rubbing his back for a few more seconds before Pranav looked up and said: 'I don't love him ... I don't love anyone. I think I am incapable of love. Just as I am incapable of finding a job.' Pranav rolled off and sat up. He straightened his T-shirt and said, 'There, I said it. You can have it all, Rishabh Malwa. Congratulations on your new job! And congratulations on getting a girlfriend. Now that you have a job, I hope she will finally allow you to fuck her.'

'You bastard!' Rishabh thundered, pulling Pranav by his shirt. He held Pranav's mouth, squeezing it tightly. Pranav flinched in fear of a blow. Once again, the image of Pranav's bruised face sprang up in Rishabh's mind. He stroked Pranav's lips with his thumb before releasing his grip. Peeling himself away from Pranav, he grabbed the bottle of beer and gulped down whatever was left in it. 'Get lost, Bhalla. Just get out of here. Before I lose it completely and knock the stuffing out of you.'

'That's your problem, Rishabh. You are spineless. You can't even admit to what is so fucking obvious,' Pranav said.

Rishabh dropped the bottle and pounced on his friend, holding his head firmly in his hands. 'Just shut up, Bhalla. I beg of you, just shut up!' he said before sealing Pranav's mouth with a passionate kiss.

Neither of them had ever experienced such a kiss. Pranav had never felt as powerful. The moon would have sprung out of its orbit and danced for him tonight if he had commanded so.

Rishabh had never felt as light as he felt right now. This was the most candid, sincere admission he had ever made. Through the kiss, he had eloquently said everything he could not ever have found the right words to express, without sounding ridiculous or mushy. They continued their intense, urgent exploration of each other's mouths, slow sucking of the tongues and this mild chewing of the lips.

What followed next seemed so natural and inevitable – the warmth of their bodies pressed against each other; the soft squeals of joy Rishabh let out when Pranav gnawed at his neck; the tight-lipped, closed-eyed exultation on Rishabh's face as Pranav's tongue traced its way from his chest to the navel and further down; the twinge of pain, made bearable only by the consuming desire that Pranav felt when Rishabh made his way inside him the first time, slowly, tenderly, stroking Pranav's back, showering it with gentle kisses.

The big rusty metallic room cooler rumbled on.

Tonight too, I sit to unload the squalor of my thoughts onto this paper. Must the paper not resent me?

It's not the big things that weigh you down – well, not always. It is the small things that nettle more. What makes it worse is that you cannot open up to others about them. In the eyes of others, they do not merit crabbing. For they are part of life – these little things. And they have to be experienced.

Every now and then, you shut your eyes, straighten your back, square your shoulders, heave a deep sigh and say to yourself: 'I shall not lose it. Okay, let's take it on. One small thing at a time.' And you do. You do so until you live. Or you live until you do so. It's these small things, trivial as they are called, that can be life-threatening if allowed to grow on you, if not battled day in and day out.

Trivialized, these little things cling to each of us and collude with those clinging to our loved ones, forming a web out of which it takes nothing less than a lifetime to escape.

The three-headed and ten-headed monsters are to be slain only in the world of fantasy; in real life it is these tiny gnats that are enough to drive you to extinction. Such a death is quite unheroic. Most deaths are quite unheroic. And we blame the wars and the epidemics. Is it fair?

Is it fair that these small struggles neither earn you sympathy when they persist, nor do they earn you praise when they are overcome? Yet, a chief part of our lives is spent wrestling with these matters which we have the gall of calling 'trivial'.

You say to yourself – okay, let's take it on. One little thing at a time.

The Anniversary

THEIR TENTH WEDDING anniversary was the day Neera decided to finally tell Kishor that she wanted to end their marriage. While her husband lay next to her snoring, she lay in her bed, awake, flitting back and forth in her mind, imagining various scenarios that might present themselves if she decided to proceed.

Kishor, in one such scenario, is helping her with the dishes in the kitchen, when she tells him. He initially mistakes the announcement for a joke, laughing freely, like a carefree man who isn't bothered by anything. Typical Kishor: laughing at all his problems as if it would make them go away. Always. But when he realizes that she was serious, he collapses on the kitchen floor, leaving her scrambling to revive him.

In the second scenario, after learning Neera's decision, Koel, Kishor's daughter, calls her a bitch and files a case of mental harassment against her. Neera knew Kishor himself would never do something as drastic. He loved her and lacked the perseverance needed to pursue legal action. Koel, on the other hand, had a mean streak. She had never shown genuine affection for Neera after all these years. Despite Kishor's repeated requests, she continued to call her 'Neeru aunty,' rather than 'mummy'. Neera, who had never imagined herself as a mother or being addressed as one, had never dared to make such a request. Even if Koel had agreed to act on her father's demand, Neera might have stopped her after a month or so. But the opportunity never came along. So, she resented Koel for depriving her of the pleasure of saying *no*, of appearing to be the bigger person, of convincing her that she did not want to replace Koel's late mother, of flaunting her emotional security while exposing Koel's lack of it.

In a different scenario, Kishor goes silent for the first three days after learning of Neera's decision. He begins avoiding her after that, pretending she doesn't exist in his life. He leaves for work before she wakes up and returns late at night, reeking of alcohol. After a few days of observing this set routine, when Neera insists on discussing their marriage, he just glares at her with such visceral disgust that it compels her to kneel and beg for his forgiveness. Looking at Neera weeping hysterically, he softens and asks her to take a deep breath and fetches her a glass of water. As she sits across from him, wiping her tears and sipping water, trying to regain her usual grace, he argues that in fact she did not want an out from the marriage. All she wanted was a little attention, which he might have failed to give her while he was busy making arrangements for Koel's departure to the United States. The look on his face says he finds it incredible that a woman her age could even consider such a thing. 'How could you, Neeru! And you chose our anniversary to bring this up, of all days,' he says, shaking his head in disappointment.

Suddenly, she snapped out of her reverie. Kishor was stirring in the bed. She got up and went to the kitchen to make tea. On the table she saw his untouched plate of food. He must have eaten out, she concluded. She transferred the contents of plate into a garbage bag and sealed it before proceeding to place it next to the main door from where it could be picked up. But then standing at the threshold, she remembered how their next-door neighbour, Paromita, had made a scene last week when the municipal worker skipped their building, leaving their trash beside her door until Neera and Kishor returned from work. She didn't want to argue with her obnoxious neighbour on the day she was about to end her marriage. So, she carried the trash back into the kitchen. She could give it to the municipal worker when he came; it was a Sunday, after all.

But why hadn't Kishor eaten last night? He'd been eating very little lately. He had also been distracted. Whenever she inquired, he replied, 'Nothing to bother you with, Neeru.' She put it down to Koel's relocation to California. He was attached to his daughter, she knew. And she adored him all the more for it. She wondered how he would have spoilt their own children if she hadn't decided against having them. Unlike her father, Kishor would have been an involved parent, albeit not as effective as an authority figure. That was Kishor. He couldn't stop himself from being a part of something, even if it meant screwing it up. For example, he purchased four different kinds of pickles for Koel to take with her. She knew Koel wouldn't take any of them. He knew too. But he still brought them for her. He tried to be stern while asking Koel to pack them in her luggage. Of course, it wasn't going to work, as it had never before. Koel had studied engineering and was now going to a foreign country for a master's degree, both against her father's wishes. They knew she'd never return. Perhaps that was why he had been so quiet lately.

As she watched the dried tea leaves fervently dance in the water, a stray thought crossed her mind: what if Kishor was having an affair? How insulting would it be if she discovered today that her husband was secretly having an affair all this while. She would never do that to him. She would never insult ten years of their companionship like this. Even now, as she stood in the kitchen, on this languid Sunday morning, trying to make up her mind about announcing the separation, she was certain that she did not want to abandon Kishor for another man. Perhaps for an imaginary man, a nameless, faceless possibility. But not a real one.

As the tea came to one boil after another, taking on a deep colour, giving off a rich aroma, the absurd idea of his affair blew off with vapours arising out of the tea. Duplicity also demands a degree of finesse which, she thought straining the tea into cups, Kishor did not possess at all. The newspaper landed on the balcony with a thud, tightly wound in a rubber band. That should jolt him awake. Thankfully, he was still sleeping. She shuffled around the kitchen, lugging the guilt of wanting to leave Kishor – something that no one, not even her friends, would understand. Kishor was not the type of man whose wife could divorce him. His wife could die, as his first wife did, or elope with a lover, but she could never divorce him.

What profanity! She wasn't twenty-five anymore. Even at the age of twenty-five, she had difficulty finding a match. Not that she didn't have suitors back then, but none who could make her laugh. None who could let her retain her last name after marriage. None who could accept a wife unwilling to mother his children. None who could not feel insecure of her charm and beauty. ('If you want, you could teach at an all-girls school; my parents will not object. Teaching is best suited for women,' one of her suitors once said.) She had given up hope of finding a suitable partner who shared her values. And then she had met Kishor.

He was an unusual choice: a widower from Delhi whom everyone in the office secretly mocked; the man with few hair and too many teeth, which stood out prominently when he laughed, deeply, generously. Was that everyone's problem with Kishor? The fact that he always seemed to be happy for no apparent reason. Did people envy his cheerful demeanour? A man whose wife had died, leaving him with a teenage daughter to raise on his own. A man whose job was in jeopardy. A man who looked the way he did. And he was still happy? No wonder people mocked him behind his back.

Despite this, he had managed to win over Neera. Neera had been drawn to him since the first time she laid eyes on him. His eccentricities intrigued her. Not only had he charmed her, but he had also persuaded her that the wild lifestyle she desired was neither sustainable nor even half as romantic as she had imagined – a feat that even her parents, when they were alive, could not manage. He had successfully convinced Neera that they must get married for her benefit, not his. Eventually, Neera discovered that, while her colleagues mocked this goofy purchase manager from Delhi who visited every two months, they could never find a concrete reason to dislike him. They made fun of him because they couldn't understand him. And the more she got to know Kishor, the more she realized how unlike other men he was. For example, he had no problem with her keeping her last name, which she then gave up within a year of marriage. Kishor, unlike the other men she knew, was not afraid of losing to her. His confidence did not border on bravado; rather, it sprang from a sense of inadequacy that was at peace with itself.

He never complained about anything, not even his sometimes disobedient but brilliant daughter, their tiny government-allotted quarter, or his own unremarkable life. Every night, after returning from work, he would shower and douse himself in talcum powder, slip into his white vest and pyjamas, and pour himself one drink too many. Every night, without fail. Not a word of complaint in all these years.

She searched the refrigerator for something she couldn't recall. Had they run out of eggs? She remembered buying them with other groceries the night before. They must be on the table. Kishor would have put everything in place if he had returned home earlier. That is why she adored him: He cleaned up the mess she made. In the house. In everyday life. He always knew how to get her out of all the trouble that her sharp tongue often got her into. He organized her life for her, establishing priorities and putting things in their proper places. All Neera had to do was stand beside him.

She cracked four eggs into a bowl, and began whisking. On their anniversary last year, he gave her an egg beater that had conked off. He liked his omelette plain. Should she chop a small onion for herself? Did she resent her acute awareness of his flaws because she envied how he ignored hers?

She ruminated over facing Koel after disclosing her decision. The word 'bitch' and its many variants swirled around in her head, making it difficult to focus on chopping the onion. Koel's small, angular face, which she had inherited from her mother (Kishor's was round and blunt) swam into her mind. It was contorted with bitterness.

Did she too believe Neera and Kishor were ill-matched? Perhaps she had never understood why Neera married her toothy, clumsy father? No, of all people, Koel knew her father's enormous capacity to love. Love that sometimes felt like a velvet leash around Neera's neck – but a leash, nonetheless. After her mother's death, Koel had never lived with Kishor. She lived with her grandmother before moving to Pune for studies and now she was shifting to the US. It was quite clear: she needed her stepmother to sponge away some of the overwhelming *Kishorness*. Then what right did she have to judge Neera? She did not stop loving her father because they stopped living together. Why would she think Neera did not love Kishor because she had decided to separate?

But did she really suspect Koel would think Neera did not love him or was that her own fear? She wondered if that was why she was crying. She loved Kishor. Her love for him may not have gurgled with a rush of hormones in her blood; instead, it had quietly seeped into her bones. She had come to know him as intimately as she knew her body. No, he had come to *be* her body. She was grateful to him for the form and shape he gave to her life. But when they were together, she could not be everything and be everywhere – did she resent that?

Of course she wasn't crying. The onion was stinging, she told herself, as she dabbed her eyes with the sleeve of her kurta. It was true that she had to come to know him as intimately as she knew her body, like she knew the nooks and corners of this small house of theirs. And as with her body, and as with this house, she was not content with her marriage either. There was something wanting. Like her body, like this house, it wasn't ideal – no, it wasn't like that of others.

The sound of taps running in the bathroom meant that Kishor was awake. It was unusual for him to wake up this late, though. She knew the routine now: a round of loud and embarrassing noises would follow as he cleaned his mouth, cleared his throat, blew his nose. After finishing, every morning, he would come out and grin at her. And that's how she knew he had woken up happy. Unlike her, Kishore didn't wish her good morning as a ritual; he meant it sincerely. Putting his arm around her shoulders, he would squeeze them gently and ask if she had slept well. Next, he would collect the newspaper from the balcony and spend half an hour reading it, making different faces, without a word. He would then ask her if she needed any help in the kitchen, though she would turn him down. She did not like the mess he created every time he entered the kitchen. But she also loved it when he cooked for her. Sometimes she pretended to be caught up at work till late, so that he would cook. Of course, she grumbled while cleaning up the next morning, but the food was delicious, though oilier and spicier than their usual meals.

Kishor was sloppy, like an unpunctuated sentence. Confusing. And even on the occasions his ways made sense to her, they lacked elegance or poise. He carried on wearing clothes without caring how they looked on him. He chewed food with his mouth open, even on their monthly fine-dining night when he recycled all his old jokes, as Neera looked around to check for onlookers.

Kishor had taught her the word *phulka* for rotis. At first, she had resisted all the Delhi-flavoured influences, but then, she had grown used to them, and eventually started enjoying them. Phulka was a prettier word than roti, and it always reminded her of the amusement with which she watched rotis puff up like a ball when her mother placed them directly on the flame. She could not evoke much pleasure in teaching him her Maharashtrian ways though. His ex-wife was also from Mumbai and had tried that already. But still, whenever Neera wanted to make *bhakhri* and *bharta* for dinner, he would say, 'Make it, Neeru, just don't break my neck with it,' and laugh.

As she placed a fresh cup of tea on the table for Kishor, she realized what had gone missing from their marriage: he had stopped telling her things. Things about the world as he saw it, about life as he bungled through it, but most importantly, things about herself. 'You are not as brave as you pretend to be, Neeru. It's okay to not be brave all the time,' he had told her within a month of her marriage, sitting on the same chair Neera was sitting on right now. She had just stood next to him pouring milk into her bowl of cereal, while thinking of a rejoinder. He was right. She wasn't as brave. She did not mind being called a bitch, but she feared actually being one.

She was going to ask her doting husband on the day of their anniversary for a divorce. What would she say when he asks for a reason? She could dismiss others, maybe even Koel, by saying it was none of their business, but Kishor? It was his business. He was the business.

He came out, his face washed but eyes still baggy. He faintly smiled at Neera but did not say anything. He quietly sat at the table and began looking for something.

'The tea is hot, be careful,' she said, as she handed him the newspaper.

'Good morning, Neeru,' he said, pouring the tea in the saucer.

'The omelette is ready too. Do you want it right away?'

'Why didn't you wait for me? You love my omelettes, don't you?'

'It's okay, Kishor. You can take care of the dinner if that makes you happy.'

'You make me happy, Neeru. Nothing else makes me as happy as seeing you sleeping next to me every night. Happy anniversary, love.'

'You remembered?'

'Have I ever forgotten?' Kishor asked earnestly.

Neera was embarrassed that she even asked. He had never forgotten in all these ten years. She was sure he had even made the booking for a dinner at their favourite restaurant.

'Kishor, I have to talk to you about something.' Neera said, cutting the omelette into two pieces and sandwiching a piece between two slices of bread. She found her hands trembling. 'I have been debating with myself for a very long time, but I cannot keep it within me anymore.'

'Neeru,' Kishor set his saucer down. 'I know what you want to say. I have been distant of late and have not been able to give you time. But, you see, I can explain. I too have something to tell you.'

'No, I know you have been busy arranging things for Koel's departure; that's not the problem. Your daughter deserves all your attention. That's why I've not asked any questions about your coming home late, your loss of appetite, your fatigue. I know how much you love her. And believe me, that is not the problem.'

'Let me finish, Neeru. It's important you listen carefully to every word of what I am going to say.' He set aside the newspaper. 'You know, sweetheart, sometimes the best suited people have to part ways. Sometimes life just can't stand two people who love each other deeply being together.'

Neera watched Kishor, her brows furled. Had the anniversary made him philosophical? Or worse, perhaps this was a long prelude to another rehashed joke. Of all things, she could not digest a joke at this moment. But then, she thought, the joke could be clinching evidence which she could use to prove that Kishor did not take anything seriously – not her, not their marriage, not even his life. She could no longer be with someone who lacked seriousness, even if she was ten years too late in admitting it.

'I don't understand, Kishor. What are you trying to say?'

'Darling, I am trying to say no bond is permanent. Even the strongest of marriages reach an inevitable end. And we need to start reminding ourselves of this reality. Nothing is permanent. This may not be the best time to talk about it, but then I thought, why not today? You should know that I have made all necessary provisions for you and Koel. You will finally be able to move to a bigger, better house. Koel and I will be out of your life.'

Neera's chest tightened. 'Kishor, are you moving to California with your daughter?'

Kishor smiled faintly. Not the way he usually did, the way that gave Neera an illusion of normalcy and comfort – this time, in his smile there was a flicker of despair.

Escape

GOODBYES WERE HARD for Rishabh Malwa. As he boarded the bus in Jaipur, his eyes were wet. He was on his way home to Delhi after his final exams. His classmates, who had planned an outing later that night, had asked him to stay back – it would be the last outing together of the 2008 batch. But Rishabh knew that after boozing, he would not be able to hold back his emotions. So he made up an excuse and got on the first bus to Delhi after the exam. He had already packed most of his belongings the night before, and the little he had left behind he could trust Pranav and Namit to keep safe. His flatmates had refused to join him on this hasty retreat; they wanted to stay back for one last outing with their batchmates before returning to Delhi.

He took a window seat in the last row. As the bus began to snake through the narrow roads of the walled city of Jaipur, Rishabh recalled the past four years. It was impossible for him to even imagine the four years without Pranav and Namit, who were inseparable from his college experience. He imagined them laughing, singing, dancing with their classmates. Namit was the clumsiest dancer he had ever seen. It was always Pranav who stole the show on the rare occasions that he danced. He was positive Pranav would dance tonight. It occurred to him, at this moment, more than anything else, he missed his two closest friends.

Who was he kidding? He missed Pranav, only Pranav. He would have been equally desolate amidst all his friends if Pranav had decided to take off instead. Of course, Rishabh would have never let him go in the first place. He would have gone to the lengths of hiding Pranav's luggage, or emotionally blackmailing him, or done something altogether different – perhaps even striking him – to prevent him from leaving. Yes, there was no other way of putting it: it was Pranav whom he missed the most on this lonesome journey back home.

Outside, the noose of darkness tightened around the ancient Aravalis. His first task upon reaching Delhi, he decided, was to convince Pranav's parents to allow their son to move in with him. He started thinking of arguments and assurances in his mind.

The farewell had reminded him of how difficult it would be to say goodbye to Pranav again. A boy for whom, unbeknownst to himself, his feelings had secretly assumed a shape he could not even identify. A shape so abstract, so absurd, so aberrant.

The first time it happened, they had both been drunk and had got into a scuffle. It was the alcohol that had blurred the fine lines between friendship and passion. The second time, too, they were drunk. But eventually, the alcohol became redundant; the edges of desire grew sharp enough to shear the overlay of inhibitions.

This desire had first sprouted as a tiny, irritating nubble in Rishabh's throat (when he noticed Pranav flirting with a dashing senior); it then expanded into a shapeless vapour that filled his broad chest (when Pranav demolished the arguments of Rishabh's girlfriend with aplomb in an intra-college debate); and then (as his lips met Pranav's for the first time), it turned into a warm fluid that gushed to his loins, firing them up.

They went on living their lives as any two close friends sharing the same roof would. Every day, they would do almost the same things: curse the college management, squabble about the interface design of their final-year project, discuss the tepid state of the economy with a rather dispiriting and somewhat inscrutable term 'global recession' looming large over their futures. All their peers knew that Rishabh and Pranav were oblivious to others when they were together. The news of Rishabh's breakup with Anjana had also spread. It was only natural for him to spend all of his free time with Pranav.

No one noticed any change, not even Namit, the third wheel of the trio. Except, of late, Rishabh had been frequently sleeping in Pranav's room. He had a perfectly legitimate reason: his room-cooler had stopped working, and Pranav's room was air-conditioned thanks to his doting parents.

Namit, however, did not notice that this was not the first time the cooler had malfunctioned – it was almost a monthly ritual. Every time it broke down, Rishabh fixed it and then bragged about it for days. This time, he said that he had given up because it was their last summer in Jaipur anyway.

The days were all the same. The three of them would banter, argue, laugh and loaf as always. It was only the nights that had begun to hum a different tune, a tune that only

Rishabh and Pranav could hear. Often when Pranav would watch Rishabh sleep next to him, spent, one arm curled around Pranav's body and the other splayed out, he would marvel at the peculiar nature of the bond that had come to form between the two of them.

Even though he had never admitted to Rishabh or even to his own self, Pranav knew Rishabh was in love with him. He also knew Rishabh was not used to *this* kind of love. Rishabh was not attracted to Pranav because he was a boy, but at the same time, he could not stop himself from loving Pranav *just because* he was a boy. He pitied Rishabh's helplessness.

But for Pranav it was wickedly amusing too. He knew Rishabh would never name their arrangement. Naming it would make it more tangible, more illicit. Pranav would crack a smile, recalling how this boy lying next to him, breathing in rhythmic cadences that could be felt, dreaming of things unknown, called him 'bro' in their daily banter at the college, even when they were alone. ('You suck at calculations, bro!'). The word would fall out so casually, so naturally, so intimately. The same tongue that, minutes before, had been wildly exploring Pranav's body, could not address him any other way. How droll it was!

The first time Rishabh fell in love, he was six.

His father had brought home a cockatoo one evening. They named it 'Kakoo', perhaps a close approximation of the word cuckoo. Little Rishabh, who had never owned an animate toy before, was obsessed with his new friend. He would spend hours watching the bird as it hopped from perch to perch, pecked at the grills of the cage, bobbed its head playfully and ate the guava bits. The TV must have felt slighted, for Rishabh would rush to meet Kakoo and feed it leftovers from his tiffin box after returning from school. Within a month, Kakoo recognized Rishabh and started jumping and chirruping in anticipation of Rishabh's return every day. They would talk in their respective languages, neither bothered to understand the other. Exchanging sweet nothings, they would tease each other and even bicker at times. The mutual pleasing, teasing and then appeasing: it *had* to be love.

On one Sunday evening, Rishabh's parents returned home after shopping for groceries to find Rishabh sobbing hysterically. Pressing his face hard against his mother's bosom, Rishabh cried bitterly. His father rushed to the kitchen to fetch a glass of water while his mother tried to calm their son.

'Rishabh, what happened, my baby? Please tell Mummy. What happened?' Anita asked.

More wails. More jerks. An inexorable outpouring of grief.

'Babu, tell me what's wrong? Do you have a stomach ache?'

There was no reply.

'Did you break something?'

The sobs amplified. So maybe he had broken something valuable. Could it have been the new music system she had asked him to stay away from?

On the morning Rishabh arrived at Pranav's house, he wore a curious smile. He had not disclosed his plan to Pranav yet. All he had said was that he wanted to meet his mother.

Rishabh was moving to Hyderabad to work at Satyam Infotech, one of the biggest IT companies in India. Pranav, on the other hand, had not been able to land a job offer on the campus and was distressed.

After enjoying the warm hospitality offered by Mrs Bhalla and thanking her for it, heaping abundant – even if not entirely sincere – praise on the home-made biscuits, Rishabh urged Mrs Bhalla to listen to him with all her attention because he had a proposal to make. Pranav's heart began to thump. He sat listening intently to Rishabh's persuasive arguments beside his mother as the tea turned cold. Rishabh had a way of speaking that sounded obsequious but unselfish – putting the listener under the illusion of having all the power when, in reality, it was the reverse. In Jaipur, he had used the same tactic with their landlord. 'The IT companies in Hyderabad hire in dozens every day, aunty. Like we hire the labour for construction work. Believe me, Pranav will get a job within a month. He can stay with me for as long as he needs. I will take care of him, don't worry. I am just speaking out of concern for him. What do I stand to gain from this?'

Once Rishabh's speech was over, Pranav was partly relieved and partly surprised. He agreed to this arrangement because it saved him the embarrassment of facing his parents and their friends every day while being unemployed. He was even inclined to trust Rishabh's conviction.

However, unlike his mother, he was not naïve enough to believe Rishabh's generous proposal was entirely selfless. Pranav knew that Rishabh had grown addicted to him, and like any other addict, he assumed he had complete control over himself and his actions.

Pranav told himself that if he gained nothing in the next three months, he would try to study filmmaking, for which he *had* to stay away from his parents' gaze. All in all, this scheme seemed profitable for him.

When little Rishabh did not stop crying, Anita began to grow worried. 'It's okay, sweetheart, stop crying now. It's absolutely fine,' she said, looking to her husband for help.

'Here, champ, drink some water and sit up straight. Stop weeping now. What did you break? Is it the music system? We will get it fixed. Take this glass, come on!' his father said, trying to mask his disappointment – after all, the music system was expensive. He went to his bedroom to examine the damage. But there was not even a scratch on the music system. After thanking God, he shouted from the room, 'Anita, the deck is fine; there's nothing wrong with it. Ask Rishabh to stop crying.'

'He is still sobbing, Girish. Come and help me.'

Rishabh's father instinctively went to the veranda to check on Kakoo. The cockatoo had been oddly silent, despite the commotion in the house. There, he discovered the source of his son's inconsolable anguish. An empty cage lay with its door unlatched. 'Anita, Kakoo has flown away ...' he cried.

After being consoled and cajoled, Rishabh finally explained what had happened. Kakoo had kept clawing at the door of the cage, wanting to play. The previous day, Rishabh's teacher had told him that it was cruel to cage birds because they liked to fly. Rishabh panicked. What if Kakoo had forgotten to fly because he was out of practice? So, after his parents left, he decided to let the cockatoo out and play with it in the room. At first, Kakoo stayed inside the cage. Then he came out warily and hopped around Rishabh for some time, eating the melon seeds Rishabh had brought. But when Rishabh tried to hold him, the bird flew away. Oh, how could he! Without even looking back once? Just like that?

'Kakoo flew away because you did not let me keep the cage in my room. You said he needs to look at the sky. Look what has happened now! If it were in my room, I could have shut the door. It's because of you that I lost Kak—' His words faltered as he dissolved into tears again.

'It's because you opened the door of the cage that the bird flew away, you idiot!' his mother wanted to say, but looking at his state, she desisted. 'I am sorry, baby. Mummy is really sorry. Now stop crying.'

Two months had passed since Pranav moved to Hyderabad, but he was yet to find work. He had got some offers from BPOs and a few unpaid internships, but none of them interested him. With every passing day, his patience was wearing thin. But at least he had Rishabh's support.

Rishabh encouraged him to find other ways to use his time productively. He was the one who convinced Pranav to join coaching classes for MBA entrance tests, explaining how the global recession of '08 had impacted the IT industry and how getting an MBA degree might put him in an advantageous position once the recession gets over and companies start hiring again. Pranav had not wanted to study engineering four years ago and he did not want to get an MBA now, but because going back to Delhi would mean leading a false life his parents, especially his father, would want him to lead, he decided to take Rishabh's advice.

It was at the coaching class that Pranav met Karthik, a married man in his late twenties. At first, he could not make sense of Karthik's knowing looks and thin-lipped smile. He thought about discussing his behaviour with Rishabh during one of their late-night conversations, but he soon figured out the reason behind the mysterious smiles.

It turned out that the previous month, Karthik and Pranav had briefly chatted with each other on Planet Romeo. Pranav had stopped responding after a week or so when Karthik, whose name and face were hidden on his profile, had asked questions that Pranav found absurd. So, when Karthik introduced himself as 'that guy from PR,' he felt embarrassed.

'How did you know it was me? My face is pixelated in the pictures,' Pranav asked. When Karthik approached him at the bus stop after the class.

'Your bag and watch gave you away.'

'But anyone could own this watch and bag. How could you be so sure?'

'That's why I asked you. And now I am sure,' Karthik said. He shifted his bag from the left shoulder to the right and glanced around. 'Would you mind a cup of tea? I know you like tea. I don't bite, you know.'

Pranav was wary initially, but Karthik seemed gentle and harmless, if a little strange.

He did not want to drink tea. Nonetheless, to quell his curiosity, Pranav decided to stay for a while, not so much to find out more about this man, as to unravel how much this man knew about him. By the time they were done, they had finished six cups. Karthik, it turned out, was even more shy and reticent than he was. All Pranav could gather was that Karthik worked as a deputy sales head at a pharmaceutical firm. He had got married at a young age, as was customary in his family. His hatred for his bossy and rude zonal head had driven him to these coaching classes. He believed that an MBA would open new doors for him.

Little Rishabh lost all zeal for life after Kakoo flew away. His silence became a cause of worry for his parents. He did not eat properly and would often stand on the balcony, gazing upwards, hoping that Kakoo would return somehow. At his mother's insistence, who could not bear to see her only child in this state, his father brought home a new bird.

Rishabh was ecstatic. His eyes shone with happiness, and he shrieked with joy when he saw the new bird for the first time. This time, the bird was named Coco. Coco was more colourful, chirpier than Kakoo. Soon, Rishabh fell in love again, with greater enthusiasm and hope. Coco would not betray his friendship, he knew. He would be his best friend.

Occasionally, Rishabh's parents were bothered that he did not go out to play with his friends as frequently as other children his age; with dread, they concluded that their son was an *introvert*. One night while discussing him, Rishabh's mother even used the i-word, not without some degree of hesitation. 'Relax, Anita. He is just a kid. Don't label him just yet. He will grow wings soon.' Girish pressed his wife's hand and patted it gently.

After just a few days, Rishabh started persuading his father to release Coco from his cage. He swore that the bird wouldn't escape, claiming Coco had told him that he wouldn't. 'He just wants to play with me, Papa. I swear he won't fly!' It was decided that Coco would be let out of the cage in Rishabh's room for some time on Sundays, under the supervision of his parents after shutting all the doors and windows.

Thus passed many sweet Sundays. Outside his cage, Coco was not restless. The bird would glide along the length of the room with an eye of an explorer. Sometimes, Girish would walk with the bird perched on his arm to amuse little Rishabh. By and by, the Malwas were assured of Coco's loyalty. Meanwhile, the bond between Coco and Rishabh grew stronger. Now the family would let the bird out even on weekdays without any care. Coco displayed no desire to leave the comfort of the Malwa household, until one fateful day.

'But you've always known that you are ...?' Pranav hesitated to complete the question. He was on the pillion while Karthik rode the bike.

'I think so. I mean, I'd never heard the term before, but as a kid, I had crushes on Sanjay Dutt and Anil Kapoor. At first, I thought I was obsessed with film stars. After an intimate experience with my cousin, it became clear it was not just the stars; rather, it's in my stars.' Karthik laughed. Somehow, his hair stayed in place despite the wind. This was the third time they were going to the Moula Ali after their evening class.

Unlike Rishabh, Karthik never shut his eyes during sex. His experience pleased Pranav. It felt good, after all, to be intimate with an *insider* – someone who had learnt, practised and mastered the tricks of the trade. With him, Pranav was discovering things about his own body that he had never known before. Also, unlike Rishabh, Karthik was completely malleable and offered himself up for Pranav. It wasn't that sex with Rishabh wasn't enjoyable, but the rhythms and contours never changed, and the roles were too set.

Pranav was fascinated by the melancholy of his dusky face. There was something oddly magnetic about his occasional stutter, his pregnant silences. Karthik was one of those rare people who evoked a protective instinct in Pranav. It was only during sex that Karthik seemed to resemble the man on his Planet Romeo profile. In bed, Karthik was animated – and occasionally even loud – in sharp contrast to his reserved and silent self otherwise.

Karthik barely spoke when they were together, which sometimes made Pranav doubt if he liked his company at all. But whenever he stopped responding to Karthik's texts, he would receive a string of messages from him. Deleting them one by one, he would feel reassured of his charm. As more time passed, Pranav realized, Karthik's silence too was his defence, his confession.

Tightly wound in the same loaded silence, they reached the hilltop and stood leaning against the stone railing of the dargah, their frequent meeting point. Like two mice looking down from a lofty tabletop. The city of Hyderabad, a vast and uneven carpet, with intricate patterns interspersed with tufts of green, laid out beneath the table. The sun had almost faded, the railing still radiated heat.

'Pranav, can I ask you something?' Karthik broke the silence.

'Sure.'

'Why did you stop responding to my messages on the website?'

'Well,' Pranav began, 'you were not willing to share pictures. You were nervous, I guess? Also, frankly speaking, I found your questions a bit strange.'

'Why? What's wrong with being curious about someone's background?' Karthik frowned.

'There's nothing wrong with it. I mean, I know my *gotra* and suchlike,' Pranav said, tilting his head to one side. 'Actually, that's not true. I asked my mother after that day. Now I know it. It's Kashyap. But that's beside the point. It's strange for someone on Planet Romeo to ask about your gotra, don't you think?

'I disagree. I think it shows they are genuinely interested in you. Maybe if I hadn't asked, you'd have never known your gotra.'

'I am not saying there's anything wrong. But I don't even understand why and how it is relevant in our times.' Pranav shrugged. 'I don't know; you may disagree with me. I still think it's weird.'

'What is wrong in being in touch with one's cultural values? Karthik asked softly. But when he saw the look of exasperation on Pranava's face, he said, 'Look, maybe it's not a subject for the here and now. I am sorry if you found my questions silly. We can talk about something else.'

'That's alright. Maybe it's a north–south thing. I never cared for these things,' Pranav said, reeling in his frustration. 'But can I ask you something?'

'Hmm ...'

'You don't really talk about your wife.' Pranav stepped back from the hot railing. 'Do you love her?'

'I like her,' Karthik replied calmly, crossing his arms. 'None of this is her fault.'

'That's not what I meant.'

Karthik feared the next question. 'Can we leave now? I have to buy some groceries on my way home,' he said in the same unsentimental way.

'Of course it's not her fault. But nor is it yours, you know? It's not your fucking fault!' Pranav wanted to scream, but he said, 'Sure, let's go.'

Anita had opened the kitchen window to clean it when Coco flew in and alighted on the kitchen countertop.

'Are you hungry, Coco?' she asked. The bird and the doorbell chirped simultaneously.

'Give me a minute,' she said, wiping her hands on her way to the door. She saw little Rishabh lying on his belly before the TV and she asked him to switch the TV off and fetch Coco lest the bird get hurt in the kitchen. 'At least look after your things, Rishabh Malwa,' she added sternly.

Before Rishabh could switch off the television, a wild cry, almost human, emerged from the kitchen. Rishabh and his mother rushed inside to find Coco crushed between the jaws of a large cat, which flounced off the window at the sight of the humans. And that is how the second love of Rishabh's life met its tragic fate.

This loss hit Rishabh harder than the first one. He had grown even closer to this bird. The shock sunk its claws in him slowly, hiding itself in a deep, inaccessible place. He ran a high fever for two days, and afterwards, his mother sensed something seriously amiss with her son. On the third night, as she kissed her son to sleep, she resolved never to get him a pet again. No, nothing that he could get emotionally attached to. She kissed him again softly.

Pranav was taken aback when Karthik invited him to his home. He had never thought a shy family man like Karthik would do something as risqué as bringing a lover home. But as he gingerly entered the house, Pranav marvelled at the intricate patterns and motifs adorning the courtyard floor. He wondered if he should ask Karthik who had drawn them.

While his gender made Pranav's pursuits outlawed in the eyes of society, he did not realize it also gave him a safety net. If found out, Pranav could easily pass off as a colleague, friend or an acquaintance of Karthik. They could have run into each other at the tea shop round the corner and forged a friendship after a discussion about the state of the country. Karthik could have discovered that they held similar political viewpoints and invited him home for some more tea. No one would so much as bat an eyelid. No one would pry. Had Pranav not been a man, however, a much lengthier explanation would be needed – none thoroughly convincing.

His estimation of Karthik's audacity was not entirely off the mark. He had been invited only because Karthik's family, including his wife, had left for Tirupati that morning. The Bhoopathys were religious people, Pranav had gathered by now.

After a long passionate interlude, they were both hungry. Karthik switched on the lights to look for their clothes. 'Get dressed while I find us something to eat. Should I switch on the geyser?' Karthik asked, hitching up his underwear.

'No. First I need some food. I am starving.' With the lights on, Pranav could see the framed pictures of Karthik and his wife on the walls. His wife was smiling ear-to-ear in all of them while Karthik wore his usual thin-lipped, reserved smile. This man couldn't even emote for a photograph. The pictures also induced a new form of guilt in Pranav. Until now, Karthik's marriage had seemed an abstract idea, and his wife, a mythical figure. But the pictures gave his guilt a name and a face. One of the pictures was their wedding photograph, which carried their names in baroque font: *Harini weds Karthik, 15th November 2004.*

Pranav imagined Karthik with his wife. In bed. The very bed on which he lay spreadeagled. Today's experience made it easier for him to imagine her. For the first time, Karthik had said he wanted to fuck Pranav. And, to Pranav's surprise, he did a very good job of it.

'Your wife is beautiful,' he said when Karthik returned.

'I know. Everyone says so. She doesn't agree, though,' Karthik said. He placed a tray loaded with fried snacks, biscuits and two tumblers of coffee on the bed.

'What do you think?'

'That doesn't really matter, does it? Women make up their own mind about these things. You try telling a woman who believes she is pretty that she is not, she will never believe you. You try telling a woman who believes she is not pretty that she is, she will never believe you either. So, I've given up.'

'You are full of surprises today,' Pranav said. The tumbler was too hot. He set it next to a slender prayer book on the bedside table. What was the point of telling Karthik that he didn't like drinking piping hot coffee from a steel tumbler anyway?

'Desperate times call for desperate measures, I guess,' Karthik said.

'Desperate times?'

'The thing is, we are trying.'

'You mean for a baby?' Pranav blew over his coffee.

Karthik nodded.

'That's nice. Kinda cute. Why do you look stressed, though?'

'Cute, maybe. But a little difficult for us.'

'Oh!' Pranav exclaimed, picking up a curious-looking snack. He wanted to ask its name, but he continued, 'Did you consult a doctor?'

'Yes, we have. And that's why I need your help,' said Karthik. He wished the lights were turned off as they were twenty minutes ago so that he could talk without being seen.

Pranav straightened his back and set down the tumbler again. For a moment he thought he had misheard Karthik. 'My help, did you say?'

'Yes, will you?'

'Karthik, I have no idea what you're talking about.' Pranav looked troubled. He already regretted asking such personal questions. Why couldn't he have left right after sex? Why had he stupidly shown interest in this person's life?

'We are looking for a donor, Pranav. A sperm donor, I mean. And you seem to be a perfect fit,' Karthik said. 'You're smart, from a good family; I know you, and the best part is – you're so fair-skinned.'

'Karthik, do you even understand what you are saying? It's sick!'

'I know it's a huge favour to ask of someone. Forgive me. But don't you see, I have no one else whom I can reach out to. Can't you try to understand my situation?'

When Pranav stayed quiet for a minute, Karthik asked, 'Do you have any Kashmiri blood in you, by any chance?'

On a Sunday afternoon, Rishabh saw Pranav fervently typing on his phone.

'All well, Bhalla? You look upset. Is something wrong?' Rishabh asked.

'Nothing. Just replying to my mother, who is nagging me as usual,' Pranav replied before tossing his phone aside and heading to the shower.

Once he was sure Pranav was in the bathroom, Rishabh opened the messages on his friend's phone. Indeed it was Pranav's mother asking about his job prospects. It was inappropriate to read someone's private messages, he thought, as he carefully put back the phone. But it was justified, wasn't it? After all, he was worried about his friend. He returned to watching porn on his laptop.

Then he impulsively picked up the phone again and went through the call log. One number had been dialled repeatedly. It was nameless. Pranav's recent aloofness, which Rishabh had so far attributed to his worry about lack of employment opportunities, was now gathering a different colour. He took down the number on his phone, though he was sure it was Hamid's. Then he kept back the phone on the bed, without caring how it had been placed, and lit a cigarette.

Pranav emerged from the shower, his face shaved and scrubbed, his hair wet and brushed and a towel – as superfluous as the subtitles in the porn video Rishabh was watching – wrapped around his waist (he was wearing underwear, Rishabh knew).

'Malla, I might return late tonight. Or maybe I won't come back,' he said. 'I mean, I'll come back tomorrow.'

'Why?' asked Rishabh.

'I forgot to tell you: Priyanshi and *jiju* are in town. I am going to meet them.'

'Oh, is your sister in town? You never told me. Can I come along?'

'No, what will you do? You don't like her husband anyway,' Pranav said, spraying himself with a deodorant.

'*Pagal hai kya*? I don't dislike him. I've never met him. I just said they seemed ill-matched,' Rishabh sniggered. 'At least, in the pictures.'

'I don't think it's a good idea. Why don't you just chill here? I'll try to come back early.'

'Bhalla, are you trying to avoid spending time with me?' Rishabh asked without looking up.

'Yeah, right!' Pranav laughed nervously, his eyes set on Rishabh's reflection in the mirror. He saw Rishabh smiling back at him and putting out his cigarette.

Pranav was buttoning his shirt when Rishabh walked up to him and repeated the question. '*Bol na*? Are you avoiding me?'

'Don't be an idiot, Malla. I will see you at night.' He turned to leave.

Rishabh stood too close for comfort, blocking Pranav's way. 'I was going through your call log while you were getting ready for your date.'

'What the ...' Pranav pushed Rishabh. 'You checked my phone?' He pushed his friend again, harder this time. 'Have you lost your mind, Rishabh!'

Suddenly, a tight punch knocked Pranav's face, and he stumbled. To Pranav, it felt like the hard, cold snowball that his sister had flung at him when they were children playing in Manali (he was six and she was twelve then). Once the surge of pain subsided, Pranav felt relief, not fear. It could have been worse, he thought. He was also overcome with a perverted sense of pride. Although he was physically hurt, he knew it was Rishabh who felt the more powerless right now.

'Fuck! Fuck! I am sorry. I am so sorry, bro! *Tu maar mujhe ... maar, bhenchod.*' Rishabh was on his knees, apologizing profusely.

'It's okay, Malla. Get up. It's okay.'

'I am sorry ... so sorry, Bhalla, damn!'

'Get up, Malla. I said it's fine. You have Priyanshi's number. You can call her and confirm our plans,' Pranav said, studying his face in the mirror, checking for signs of injury.

'Of course not. I am sorry. You should go, I will wait for you. I am so sorry, bro!'

'Are you sure?' Pranav asked.

'Yes, I am very sure. Go, *yaar*.' Rishabh fixed Pranav's collar and let out a sigh. 'And listen, collect the keys from Lakshmi *bamma*. I'll leave early for work tomorrow, so I'll give her the keys in case you stay the night.'

'No, don't bother the old woman. I will come back tonight. You take care, okay?' Pranav said, hugging Rishabh tightly.

As Pranav sat down to tie his shoelaces, he wondered if he should ask his sister to let him stay the night with her at the hotel. Suddenly, he was grateful he was meeting her and not Karthik (as he had been doing for the last four Sundays). Turning around, he smiled and waved at his friend who was lying on his stomach watching something on his laptop – he wondered if it was porn.

Pranav was now sure that Rishabh, helpless, powerless and madly in love, was on his way to doom. He wished he could escape the torture of witnessing his friend's unravelling. Could he prevent it? He did not know, and tonight, he didn't care. Right now, he just wanted to move away, away from the wicked pleasure of watching the helplessness of Rishabh and Karthik play out, away from the burden of emotionally supporting both of them when his own life was a wreck.

He knew goodbyes were difficult for Rishabh. After all, they were very close friends. Pranav did not want to hurt him, not with his words at any rate. He wondered if he could silently retreat from his dear friend's life. Just like that.

Shades of Love

On the day of her wedding, Harini felt it was the happiest she would ever be. She was finally going to have a home of her own, *her* home, and a new name – Harini Bhoopathy. It sounded better than her maiden name, Harini Mittapally, in her assessment. Now she could wake up early in the morning, wash the courtyard and decorate the floor with exquisite *kollam* using a paste of ground rice. She could wake her husband up every morning with a smile on her face and *gajra* in her damp hair. She could invoke all the gods with bells, lamps and sweet-smelling incense to bless her small house and its occupants. She could do all the things she had seen her mother do every morning without fail. And Harini could not have asked for a better partner.

Karthik was every bit the ideal husband she had always prayed for: gentle, good-looking, God-fearing. He had been shyer than she was when his family had come to meet her the first time. Harini had instantly liked him and had decided to marry him. From the way he smiled at her when she offered him sweet *pongal,* she knew he was willing too. It was the perfect match, her father had exclaimed. They looked like Ram and Sita together.

Despite all her excitement, Harini was nervous in the initial days of her marriage. She wanted to do everything correctly. To be anything less than perfect could reflect poorly on her parents, she thought. Thus, she started waking up half an hour earlier than she needed to; decided to observe a fast on Fridays like her mother-in-law, though it had not been asked of her; and happily bore all of Karthik's brother-in-law Vijayan's tantrums for the entire month or so that he had stayed with them after the wedding.

One night, Vijayan had demanded to be served a snack of *punugulu* with his coffee after dinner. Amma was old and now the senior. Veena *akka* was pregnant. With oily smiles and expectant faces, both the women looked at Harini. And Harini, the eager apprentice, rose to the occasion. She gracefully tucked her *pallu* around her waist and began to work in the kitchen. Mixed sounds of chatter, laughter and loud TV commercials coming from the drawing room could not distract her.

When Karthik quietly entered the kitchen and started frying the punugulus with her, she knew she had chosen the right man. At first, she protested but then fell silent when Karthik placed his hand around her bare midriff and pressed it gently. She mentally thanked Goddess Gauri for giving her a husband like Karthik, as she dropped tiny portions of the batter in hot oil, her bangles jingling lightly.

He had been so gentle with her the previous night when, two weeks after the wedding, she had finally agreed to do what she called her 'wifely duty'. Her friends had told her that men are usually impatient in these matters. But not her Karthik. He understood her apprehensions and had promised she would feel no pain at all. Although she had wanted to ask how come he was so sure as if he had done this before, she felt too nervous. So, she quietly agreed with whatever he said. He was right, as it turned out. She had hardly felt any pain. Sex had been remarkably smooth and – if she had to admit – thrilling. She had never felt a sensation so acute, either of pain or pleasure, coursing through her body. Those waves of uncanny pleasure, arising from below her navel and radiating outwards, made her breasts puff up like perfectly round punugulus that Karthik was deftly draining out of hot oil.

'I think these are enough, no? Don't add too much milk to Nanna's coffee – he likes it strong. I am going upstairs now. I have told them I have a headache,' he said softly before adding, 'Listen, come back quickly, okay?'

Harini served the fritters in a bowl and set the milk to boil for the coffee. A silly smile bloomed on her face as she placed her hand on her midriff and pressed it. No, it did not feel the same.

Growing up, Harini had seen her mother expressing concern over her dark skin. She had always yearned to be fair-skinned – more for her mother's sake than her own. She despised herself for not having inherited her mother's radiant complexion. Deep down, she felt, her mother too resented her for this gross incapacity. Harini was tall, wiry, and hollow-cheeked, like her father. Why could she never be opportunistic – even as a zygote? Why did she have to take after her father in matters of complexion and composition?

Harini believed that her dark complexion was one of the greatest obstacles to her happiness and finding a good husband. For her mother, there was no difference between the two. It was perhaps unfair to blame her mother alone, for she knew her father also harboured similar notions. Although, thanks to his city-bred demeanour, he never gave utterance to such thoughts, not in Harini's presence at least. His disappointment reached Harini mostly by way of her mother. Very early on, she had resolved that despite her dark complexion, if she got married, she would never give anyone a chance at disappointment.

She wanted to be a good daughter-in-law and wife – one who woke up early, washed the courtyard and drew beautiful geometric patterns on the floor. A wife who lit lamps, burnt incense sticks, rang bells to please the gods and prepared tasty *laddus* to fill their bellies.

When she married Karthik, Harini was just twenty-two. Four years into their marriage, her initial fervour had subsided. Though she had proven to be a good daughter-in-law, she had also learnt to overlook her own minor lapses. She did not punish herself if she overslept by twenty minutes, for instance. Now she felt it was earned. Harini had been an excellent wife to Karthik. Not a day had passed when her husband had gone to work without a home-cooked meal, which he mostly found delicious. She had dutifully tended to him when he suffered a severe bout of jaundice. In these four years, she had not made a single demand of him.

From the way Karthik treated her parents in her absence, she was confident that he was happy with her. Her mother had even said to her once that she could *see* the gratitude in Karthik's eyes. And she was generally right about these things. Harini had also realized that Karthik was as lucky, if not more, to have her in his life as she was to have him. But she still was not sure if she had been a good daughter. At times, she wondered if that was the reason she had not been able to have children of her own yet. Maybe her mother's discontentment with her, she thought, had transformed into some sort of a curse.

All the elderly women who came to visit the Bhoopathys invariably took Karthik's mother aside before leaving to tell her how blessed she was to have a daughter-in-law like Harini. Some attributed this bliss to the pious life Karthik's mother had led, while others to her devotion in her youth to her own mother-in-law. Some simply attributed it to luck. They spoke in clichés about how money can buy everything except for peace of mind or how filial obedience had become a rarity. Karthik's mother knew their admiration was an indirect way of conveying their disappointment with their own children and their spouses. A grandchild would follow very soon. It was a matter of time, they would say sympathetically. Just pray to Tirupati, they would add, before going away.

Four years ticked by, but 'good news' eluded the Bhoopathys. At first, they thought it was anxiety that was preventing her from conceiving a baby. As more time passed, her mother-in-law began to say this was God's way of testing their patience. *Their* patience, not Harini's alone. In her well-meaning way, her mother-in-law tried to make Harini feel less guilty and not singularly responsible. The thought of her son being responsible, however, never crossed her mind.

Her delusion could not last long. When she learned that Karthik and Harini had been consulting a doctor, she was shocked to hear that her son had undergone something called a fertility test whose results were impending. Initially, she couldn't even understand the mechanics of the whole procedure. How could the doctors test a man's fertility? Did they perform a test on his semen in their laboratory? But the semen couldn't be drawn out like blood, could it? Did they use a syringe?

With no other way out, Harini explained the process to her guileless mother-in-law: 'No, amma. He ejaculated in a tiny container. They tested me too. Today the doctor has called us to discuss the result. I am nervous, so you must come along with us. We can't rely on men alone in these matters.'

At the clinic, the lady doctor smiled at them warmly and asked them to sit down. Two walls of her cabin were made of glass. On the walls were framed certificates – one from a foreign university, posters of slender white women holding their plump babies and diagrams of reproductive organs with neatly labelled parts, the kind that could make a biology teacher deliriously happy.

The doctor handed over an envelope to Karthik and, with a sense of forewarning, said that there was no need to feel hopeless just yet. She then explained how the latest advances in the field of IVF could help couples like Karthik and Harini.

Karthik couldn't make much sense of the complicated terms and numbers neatly stacked in different columns under their names on the report. But from the doctor's sympathetic expression and her assurances about the clinic's success rate, he was sure there was a problem.

None of the three Bhoopathys thought it wise to interrupt the doctor during her speech. Harini wondered if Karthik was able to register all that the doctor was saying. He seemed absorbed in the report. When the doctor finally paused, Karthik took a sip from the glass of water on the table and asked his mother to wait outside. Harini gave her mother-in-law a nod of assent. Puzzled and overwhelmed, the old woman hesitantly walked out. After his mother left, Karthik said, 'Ma'am, we don't understand a lot of these technicalities. But from what I understand, we cannot have a child – naturally, I mean.'

'But there's still hope, Mr Bhoopathy. That's what I have been trying to explain to you,' the doctor replied as gently as she could.

'Of course, I understand. That's why we came here, you see. We'll think about our options.'

'Sure, give it a thought. Take your time. I know these decisions are difficult. You can always contact me if you have any questions.'

'I just have one question for now,' Karthik said.

'Go on.'

'Whose fault is it?'

Harini Bhoopathy loved her husband. Nothing was going to change that – not even the low motility of his sperms. She had considered the matter closed when the doctor had said the only way for them to have a child was through artificial insemination, which would involve a third-party donor. There was no way she could have agreed to it. She dared not even imagine the look of disgust on her parents' faces if they learned of Karthik's proposition.

But one evening, a week later, when Karthik brought up the topic of going ahead with the procedure, she was startled. She was ironing clothes on her side of the bed while Karthik pretended to read a magazine on his. 'I think you've gone crazy. Or have you started drinking?' Harini exclaimed, widening her eyes.

'Just listen to what I am saying,' Karthik replied, putting down the magazine.

'I am not listening to anything. Do you realize what you are asking for? It's like sleeping with another man.'

'Don't put it like that. It's a medical procedure. You don't have to sleep with anyone. They will just implant a donor's sperm in your womb. It will be our baby.'

'You want me to carry the child of a random stranger? A person's whose caste and gotra we don't know! What if he's not even Hindu!' Harini's hands moved furiously over the shirt she was ironing.

'There's no other way. I thought we could ask Vijayan. Veena akka won't mind. But when I asked Amma, she said no one should ever come to know about this situation, should we go ahead. No one. Not even Veena akka. Now, where else will we find a donor with the right caste and gotra without letting the world know of our problems.'

'Look, I have a lot of work on my hands. Amma's joint pain has started acting up again. I haven't even started preparing dinner. I have no time for your whims.' She picked up the stack of ironed clothes and left the room. But she was back the next minute.

'I am so silly, I forgot to take the massage oil. I don't even remember where I'd put it last. Which reminds me, please get up and oil the hinges of the door outside the pooja room. It creaks so loudly that it wakes everyone up in the morning.'

As she shuffled around the bed, holding the stack of clothes and looking for the oil, she noticed tears in Karthik's eyes. Instantly dropping the clothes onto the bed, she sat next to him. 'I am sorry. I am so sorry. But don't you see how unfeasible this idea is?' she said, taking her husband's hands in her own. She wiped his eyes and put her head in his lap. Now her own eyes were wet with tears.

'It's easy for you to say,' Karthik said. 'Because you're not the one at fault. You don't know how people will behave when they hear. I will be blamed for this. They will get more ammunition to act nasty.'

Confused, Harini sat up and wiped her eyes with her pallu. 'What ammunition? What are you talking about?'

'That's the thing, Harini. You don't understand. And you won't understand. All my cousins are fathers now. Almost all of them have at least two children. I will be singled out, like before. *Nishphalmaina*. The useless one,' Karthik said, his voice thick with despair.

'Damn your cousins and the others! I don't care what they say. You're not useless. You're my world.'

'You don't care about what others say. But I do, Harini.' His shoulders drooped and he leaned back on the bed.

Harini hadn't ever seen her husband's vulnerable side like this. It was as if she was meeting him for the first time.

It dawned on her that in all their conversations over the last four years, she had never realized how her husband mostly remained silent, hiding God knows how many stories and secrets within. Should she apologize for her negligence?

For now, she said, 'I will think about it, if it's this important to you. But what about Nanna? Who will tell him?'

'We don't have to tell anyone anything,' Karthik said. 'Nanna knows we consulted a doctor. We can say there was some issue that was fixed by medication. That's it.'

Harini returned a look that said she was not convinced. 'I must get started with the dinner.' She picked up the clothes and left the room.

Later that night, Harini sat beside her husband and asked,' Why did your cousins tease you as a kid? Is there something more you're keeping from me?'

Karthik hesitated. 'Will you be able to take it? What if you leave me after knowing it all? I won't be able to bear it.'

'I am your wife. Nothing is going to change that,' Harini placed a reassuring hand on her husband's shoulder.

Karthik wished he could capture Harini's words, frame them and hang them next to their photographs on the wall. He raised his eyes to look at her, the tenderness of her gaze comforted him. He had grown addicted to this tenderness, this comfort, in the last four years. Was it wise to put them at stake?

He rose to shut the door.

After listening to her husband's confessions that night, Harini could not sleep. She did not say anything that night and for many nights thereafter. But Karthik persisted. Every night, after dinner, once Harini had finished reciting prayers from the slim, yellowing prayer book that she always kept on the nightstand, Karthik began recounting his experiences to her. Mostly, she lay with her back to her husband, her eyes closed as she pretended to be asleep.

At first, she had felt deceived, angry and frustrated. But the more he opened up about his past, the more sympathetic and relenting Harini grew. As she had some time to process the uncomfortable truth, she understood why he had not shared his secrets with her before. 'Where was the opportunity to tell you anything before the marriage?' he asked. 'Did we ever meet for more than ten minutes unchaperoned? After the wedding, I asked myself what did I owe you more: honesty or happiness? Forgive me, I chose happiness. As time passed and we grew closer, I began to fear losing you if I revealed the truth. And I couldn't afford to lose you.'

Had Karthik told the truth on their first night together, Harini would have seen him only through the lens of the unsettling revelation. Particularly because there was nothing else she knew about this person who was now her husband. But, four years of marriage later, she had come to love this man. He was not just her husband but also a friend, a companion, a soulmate. A man who loved her for who she was and never considered her complexion or gender reasons to think less of her. He wanted her in his life and feared losing her.

Harini had never made any demands of her husband because she was never compelled to. He had taken care of all her needs material and physical without her even asking for it. Never did he make her feel less desirable. Never did she go to sleep feeling discontented after they had sex. It is also true, however, that she didn't have very tall expectations to begin with. She had learnt to be content with what she had and to be thankful for it. And once she had overcome the initial shock, this revelation felt like any other piece of information. Harini knew she would have difficulty figuring out where this new piece could fit in her life.

Karthik's stories of harassment and humiliation from childhood filled her eyes with tears. She now realized that her husband's taciturn nature was a carapace he had forged to shield himself from the cold stares and bitter remarks of his peers. How could she not express empathy? After all, as a child, she had experienced similar humiliation for something she had no control over.

When she was ten, Harini had once gone to school with her mother for a parent–teacher meeting. On the way to school, her heart swelled with pride in anticipation of all the praise her teachers would heap on her because she secured the top rank in the class. Maybe her mother would finally see her worth. Harini made her mother sit on the bench that she usually sat on. When she pointed out to her mother that her name was written on the blackboard with coloured chalk on the top, her mother smiled and looked happy. At their turn, Harini proudly escorted her mother to her class teacher's table.

The space was abuzz with activity, with a steady stream of parents flowing in and out. Teachers from other classes were also sitting in the same room. One of them smiled warmly at the Mittapallys. Harini's mother looked nervous; she had asked her husband to attend the meeting, but he was busy with an annual audit in his office. She kept tugging at her pallu, smiling and nodding at everyone who made eye contact with her, including the peon.

Harini's mother was a beautiful woman, who made her presence felt in the room against her own wish. Her kohl-rimmed eyes were liquid and expressive; her slender nose studded with a sparkling star-shaped nose pin. She had a tall, voluptuous body that was gracefully draped in a blue saree with a broad golden border, and her thick black hair was tied in a braid that reached her broad hips.

As Harini introduced her mother to her class teacher, the teacher looked pleased and startled by her mother. 'Good afternoon. We have never met before, have we?' the teacher asked.

'No. Usually, her father comes for these meetings. How is she doing in the class?' Harini's mother enquired.

'She is doing very well and ranked first this time. Congratulations!' the teacher replied. She took off her glasses and examined the saree of Harini's mother more closely. 'Where did you get this saree from? Such a fine border.'

'Her father got it when he went on an official tour last month. He travels a lot,' Harini's mother said and tugged at her pallu once again.

'Your husband is very lucky. You look so pretty. How come Harini's colour is so different from yours?' the class teacher asked.

'She takes after her father.'

'Such a pity. She is a nice girl, but she looks like she has been baked. You must keep her from playing in the sun,' the teacher said, pulling one of Harini's cheeks.

'As if she listens to me. She is just like her father, you see,' her mother replied.

Harini could not resist butting in: 'But, ma'am, I won the kho-kho championship last month.'

She knew she had spoken out of turn. Her mother glared at her.

By now, the teacher was busy calling the attention of her colleagues to Harini's mother. Soon they were all marvelling at her beauty. When her class teacher repeated how incredible it was that Harini was her mother's daughter, the others nodded vigorously in unison. Looking at her mother, who had flushed crimson, Harini realized why her mother asked her father to attend the school meets.

'You know, Mrs Mittapally, I know just the thing that can help you. It's a sure-shot remedy to improve complexion,' the class teacher said.

'Oh, I have tried all creams and remedies. The colour is stubborn. Nothing works,' Harini's mother said, her helplessness apparent in her voice.

'*Gaumootra*! Cow-urine. Nothing works like it. Many don't believe it now, but it's an ancient science. Cow-urine has acids which can burn all the melanin in the skin,' the class teacher said, handing over Harini's report card to her mother. 'Just massage the girl's face with gaumootra for fifteen minutes every morning. At night, apply a paste of pure cow-ghee and turmeric. And you'll see the difference in a week.'

A lump formed in Harini's throat, and her earlobes burned. All eyes in the room were fixed on her. Her class teacher's suggestion had sparked a new discussion among the parents and other teachers. There were a few parents who disagreed with her. While some said cow-urine should not be used for cosmetic purposes because it was holy, only one elderly man (likely a grandparent) called the idea 'complete rubbish' in English. Harini, however, had tuned out. The responses and reactions were reaching her only as a distant murmur.

A water container sat behind her teacher on a wooden stool with a tap-like opening and two inverted glass tumblers were placed next to it. Beneath the container was a small bucket made of cheap plastic, which was filled with water that trickled from the tap, drop by drop, or the leftover water that, once taken out, could neither be drunk nor put back in. Harini's eyes were fixed on the bucket. She wished she could splash its water onto the blackboard to erase every trace of her name from it. She wanted to snatch the flimsy report card from her mother and dash it on the ground to stomp on it until it was torn to bits.

Harini noticed the other girls giggling. Some rushed out with excitement to relay the episode to their other friends. She regretted waking up that morning and bringing her mother to school. It was difficult to decide whom she despised more: her class teacher or her own mother, the praises of whose beauty spread like fragrance wherever she went. The fragrance choked Harini's tiny nostrils sometimes, making it difficult for her to breathe.

For many months since that day, Harini Mittapally was teased with the name 'Harini Mootrapally' at the school.

Inside the common lavatory, right above the urinal, someone had written in a scraggy hand: 'Harini Mootrapally's Beauty Parlour.'

'You return home late frequently these days. Is there too much work?' Harini asked. Tonight, she initiated the conversation while reheating food for Karthik who had missed dinner with the rest of the family yet again.

'Yes, kind of. The new zonal manager is an ass. He wants us to slog like asses too,' Karthik said. Having washed his hands, he searched for a napkin. It was missing from its usual place, but he did not ask his wife. 'I am thinking of doing an MBA. That might help me find a better job. Did you eat anything?'

'Yes, I was hungry. Here, wipe your hands,' she said, extending her pallu. 'Amma has put all the napkins in the laundry.'

For the past few days she had been just replying to Karthik's questions in monosyllables and nods in private. But like the good daughter-in-law that she was, she did not let her marital problems step outside of her bedroom. At the dinner table, in the presence of the rest of the family, she pretended that everything between her and her husband was fine.

'Do you know there's a new Jagannath temple coming up in Banjara Hills?' Karthik tried to milk the opportunity.

'Yes, Nanna said it would be good to have one in Hyderabad. Amma won't have to go to Puri for the Rath Yatra then. She wants to pray to all incarnations of Vishnu for a grandchild apparently,' Harini said.

'It will not open to the public before another six months,' he said, sipping the *pulusu*. 'About the grandchild,' he cleared his throat and added, 'more than gods, it is in your hands, both of us know that.'

'If you tell her that, I will tell her other things that I know,' Harini snapped.

'Are you still angry with me, *priyanamma*? Set aside your anger at me and think about this calmly. Have I demanded anything of you before?' Karthik said, gesturing for more rice. 'Lord Jagannath will bless us with a son like him. We will call him Jagdish.'

'I don't like that name. I don't want a son like Jagannath,' Harini said, rising to fetch the rice bowl.

'Why? What's wrong with him? He is the Lord of the Universe,' Karthik stopped eating for a moment.

'Nothing. I just want a son like Balram. Or if it's a girl, then Subhadra,' Harini said, dishing out steaming rice.

'Um, okay, we can decide on names later. But does that mean you're willing to go ahead with the procedure?'

'No, it's not just about the names,' Harini said. 'I want a fair-skinned child, like Balram.'

At first Karthik couldn't process the remark. But the next moment, the import of Harini's demand hit him. He swallowed.

'But you know that's not possible to ensure, Harini.'

'Why, the doctor said everything is possible now!'

'I know, it's possible, but that'll give the whole game away.'

'Karthik Bhoopathy, listen to me now: if there's going to be a baby, the baby must be fair. Or I don't want a child.' This was perhaps the first time Harini had raised her voice in her four years of marriage. She was determined not to have her child experience the same shame she had faced in her childhood. Looking at the shock on the hapless face of her gentle, good-looking, God-fearing husband, she softened her tone and added, 'Have I ever demanded anything of you before?'

Karthik sipped some more pulusu.

Tonight too, I sit to unload the squalor of my thoughts onto this paper. Must the paper not resent me?

The promise of a better tomorrow, rather its illusion, drives one today. This tomorrow feeds off the hopes one raises today. Every evening the sun hides, unable to bear upon itself all the burden of hopes one invests it with as it rises. Then the night falls. Enough time for one to recover from the momentary realization that the perishing of those promises is as inevitable as the rising of the sun the following morning. Also, enough time for one to weave a new tapestry of hopes that one expects life will fulfil.

One adds a dash of that hope into tea one brews in the morning. And one opens the newspaper with the hope of finding a possibility of that promise, pressed neatly between the folds of those pages, resembling tiny ants fighting for space, materializing. The newspapers have enough material to demolish all the hopes of having such hopes; and yet one doesn't give up. With the pages of that newspaper the hope gets recycled too.

They don't make a big crashing sound as they perish, these promises. They don't go all BOOM and BAAM! They just fade away. A silent death mostly. And then, even before one is done mourning for the lost hopes, new ones start budding and replace the former. And one begins to chase the newly arisen hopes. One knows it's a bait. Yet one is drawn to it guilelessly and helplessly. Just a certain GPA, a certain degree, a certain job, an apartment with a certain number of rooms in a certain neighbourhood ... just this one thing, or that And then will commence the gilded age, one thinks. Does it, though? Even if one gets all of these and maybe more?

It's a Sisyphean task: one tries to claw their way out of this hopeless pit, and after coming out of it somehow, one finds themselves in an even deeper pit.

All of life is this: digging new pits, trying to get out of them, only to envy the pits of the others and wanting to dive into them right away, or to pity the pits of others hoping to never get pushed in those. But a pit is a pit. Hopeless pits made of hopes.

Swipe, Kiss, Repeat

After coming home from a date, I received a call from a friend to ask how it went. It was good, I replied.

'That's great! Why do you sound so low then? What's wrong?'

'Everything,' I said. 'Everything!'

Things are manageable when a date goes badly. You come home, bitch to a friend, watch some TV, gulp down a glass of wine – and by the next hour, you're back to where it all began: Tinder, Grindr, whatever.

The real trouble begins when the date goes well.

It happens quickly. You are trawling on Grindr on a Sunday when you stumble upon his profile. He's gorgeous but you skip past him because he seems too good-looking. You busy yourself with other things (other apps, I mean). But after an hour or so, you decide to ping him because, well, he is gorgeous. What's the worst that could happen: he won't reply? Big deal! Many of them don't, you think, as you type 'hi' and press enter. And of course, there's no reply. You continue chatting with other people you've been talking to for a while. There are some you wouldn't mind meeting, but they don't excite you, and there are others who you make small talk with the way you would with a neighbour if you ran into them in an elevator. Then, out of the blue, he replies to your message with a 'hey, wassup?'

His name is Pranav, and he's a documentary filmmaker. At this point, you don't bother to dig out too much information. It's just a hook up. You're not getting married to him or anything. He is not a psychopath – you've established that and that's all you need to know. You make a plan to meet. You take a cab to his place because you want to smell fresh when you reach and you are in no mood to deal with the hassle of switching between metro lines. When you arrive at the landmark he's asked you to reach, you call him up. He is guiding you through the lanes in a squeaky voice and it occurs to you that you haven't asked whether he's a top or a bottom. He sounds like a bottom, but now you've come too far, so you keep walking. There he is, waving from his balcony. The first exchange of smiles is always awkward, even though you've done this many times before.

You climb the stairs, straightening your clothes and combing your hair with your fingers as he opens the door quietly and greets you with a hello. You stand there for now, unsure of how formal or informal you're supposed to be. He apologizes for the mess in the house since it's being renovated. You smile and assure him it's fine. He offers you water, and you hold the glass, and sip when you have nothing to say. He suggests moving to his room as it will be more comfortable. You think it's a good sign that he approves of you. But what if he's only being polite and feels obligated to invite you since you've come for a hook up? You get up to move anyway.

Inside the room, he lies down on the bed with his head propped on his arm and asks you to make yourself comfortable. You're stunned by his beauty now that you've finally had a quiet moment to observe him. Within minutes, you're both naked, going for your first kiss. You kiss again. And kiss some more. For the next two hours you hardly do anything more than kissing him, as though your life depends on it. He kisses you back, madly. You both confess that you find each other very attractive. You like each other a lot and you want to say you love him, but you smother that urge with another kiss.

Suddenly, his flatmate knocks at the door, needing something – his medicines – that is in his room. Flustered, your date searches for it but can't seem to find it.

'I guess we will have to let him in and look for it,' he says.

'Do I have to get dressed then?' you ask.

'Not if you can remain inside the bathroom while he collects his stuff.'

You continue kissing until it's difficult for either of you to let go. Another knock at the door interrupts you. He looks helpless and lost. There is another knock as his flatmate shouts he will just take two minutes. You can sense the flatmate's embarrassment from his tone. Your date looks at you tenderly as if to say, 'Look what you've done! Oh, look what you've done to me!' You want to declare to the world that he is yours; overcome by a protective urge towards him, you want to smother him with your affection. 'Go to the bathroom, please,' he says. You agree, though it makes you feel like a silly teenager. From behind the bathroom door, you hear the flatmate apologizing for the interruption. Your date responds, 'It's cool. Now look for it quickly, he is waiting in the bathroom.'

In the bathroom mirror, you notice a hickey on your left shoulder. 'Marked,' he had said in the heady moment, his eyes twinkling. You wonder how you will manage this new relationship along with your work and other responsibilities. Maybe you could come to his place directly from work every Friday and spend the weekends with him. To begin with, at least. While you're lost in thought, he enters the bathroom and wraps his arms around you, asking what you're thinking. You reply, 'Nothing.'

Back in bed, he tells you he sings and records songs in his voice. He asks if you'd want to listen. You fear his taste in music will be exotic like his looks – what if it's in Persian and you can't understand or appreciate it. But instead he plays a rendition of A. R. Rahman's 'Tu Hi Re', and your heart somersaults.

By the time you reach home, you're certain you're in love. Your head is spinning with all that has happened. You replay all the moments in your head, and the more you do, the deeper you fall into the abyss. You want to confess your love for everything about him: his clear eyes, his earnest smile, his easy-going nature, his fragrant breath, the way he admitted to not being ready for love. Still, you know he desperately needs love, even if he is too anxious to see it, too scared to lose the free rein. You're petrified at the thought of someone else being in his bed the next day and wonder if he'll like the other guy better? You're reminded of a hot date he had mentioned. You hate that guy, wishing you could scratch his face, hating the fact that you're not hot. You know you can love him in ways the other guy never will. Your magical intimacy with him cannot be recreated with anyone else. The other guy would never understand why your date loves Asha Bhosle's songs more than Lata Mangeshkar's (like you do), even without spelling it out. He will never invite the hot guy to watch *Ijaazat* with him on a rainy afternoon like he'd invited you. You write a silly poem when you get home.

Monday: You are at work. But everything feels so different. You look around to see what has changed. Nothing, except that now you're in love. Love and heartbreak – within two days. You marvel at your naïveté and pity your vulnerability. You keep hoping he'll message you saying, 'Come to my place as soon as you're done with work. I loved having you over. I can't wait to have you over again in my arms, kissing you like crazy. I love you too, idiot!' No such message comes, of course. You check your phone at regular intervals to see if he's online on WhatsApp.

Tuesday: You had thought this fever would fade out. You realize it hasn't. You send him the link to an article you recently published on your blog. That should look cool, no? It doesn't say 'I love you, I miss you profoundly. Please call me again'. The piece is about why straight parents struggle to raise queer kids. It does not sound desperate, no? There's no response. The tick marks turn blue, indicating he's seen the message. Maybe he is busy at the moment, you tell yourself.

You decide to visit his Facebook profile. There he is: Pranav Bhalla, Director at QuickPlay Films, with mutual friends. You resist the temptation to click on the 'Add Friend' icon since he's clearly not interested in taking this further. You know he is afraid because he genuinely likes you. If he did not or wasn't scared, he would have sent a friend request that very night.

Or maybe you're just deluding yourself. Maybe he later realized how out of shape your body was. Those love handles, they must have stood out when you'd walked naked to the bathroom. You resolve to get rid of them.

There's a post on his wall asking if anyone is up for partying. You imagine him dancing, drunk and carefree, with others like him who go to these parties in the hope of finding hope but end up bingeing on booze and booty. Oh, but how gorgeous he must look when he dances. You wish you could be there to watch him, to hold his drink when he starts dancing, to be at his side when he wobbles back through the crowd, to ask people to back off when they make unwelcome moves and to help him into the car and drive him home.

But you're at work. There are people around you. Chattering. Your colleagues are planning a potluck lunch. They ask what you're going to bring. You look at them in disbelief. You want to tell them to shut up, for the love of God, shut the fuck up. You want to tell them that you are heartbroken. You need their sympathy, not their demands. You want to tell them you're in love with a man you've met once. You want them to laugh at you for being juvenile so you could then hate them even more. You want to tell them you're not the kind of person who feels so strongly that easily. How could they have not figured out that yet? Stretching your lips into a smile, you ask what they are discussing. Maybe you could bring some pulao, you suggest, just to make them keep quiet. But they don't. A female colleague asks if you're going to use onion and garlic in the pulao. The question is absurd, and you reply, yes obviously. She presses her lips before telling you that's not a good idea. You say, 'Ma'am, didn't you order a chicken biryani last week? How was that not a problem?' She instantly says, '*Arey*, but you see, it's *ekadashi* tomorrow. I don't eat onion or garlic on ekadashi.' They go on to discuss elaborately how many rice dishes will there be finally. You feel like running away to find a sympathetic stranger you could hug and cry. Your eyes glisten, and you ask to be excused before anyone notices your wet eyes.

Wednesday: You're still thinking about the party. You realize you're not upset only because you can't have him but because there are so many others out there who can and who will. You feel diminished. You wanted him to at least say that you were not just one of the many boys he has bedded, that you were special, that he will always remember you differently. But then you know that's what you were – a hook up. And, to be fair, you knew that when you decided to board the cab that day. With such confidence, you'd replied to his messages then, before you had locked lips with him. Look at what's become of you now.

You go to his Instagram. He is smiling into the camera with his flatmate-cum-friend. You remember he'd said that they are good friends. He'd said that he'd feel extremely uncomfortable about undressing before his flatmate. He had put on clothes every time he'd opened the door to let his friend in – the first time to let him look for his medicine and the second to pay for his share of labour charges (they were getting the flat renovated, which is why you had to use the flatmate's room). You'd asked him if it's difficult not to get attracted to someone when you share the same space physically and emotionally.

He had suddenly grown pensive. Was it an inappropriate question? No – he'd shaken his head. It had just reminded him of his flatmate from college, Rishabh Malwa, who had died by suicide after jumping out of their seventh-floor window. ('He just leapt out of the window. Like a novice bird attempting to fly! Of course, he landed on the floor with his skull cracked open.') You had seen how sad this memory had made him. You had kissed his forehead. 'I learnt my lesson. Since then, I just share the flat. No mating,' he had said with a wink. You recall how your heart had raced at the wink and his smile. But you collect yourself. So with this one, he is only friends, just another *bro*.

Bros talk about dates, you think. He must have discussed you with his flatmate. There's no way the flatmate would not have asked about the date. What if you message the flatmate to find out if they discussed you. He's tagged in the picture. In seconds, you've landed on his profile. He is called Kul Luthra. You begin framing the message in your head: '*Hi Kul, I hope you remember me?*' No, that sounds incorrect. He is not obliged to remember you, given you'd not even exchanged greetings with him. You had silently slipped away downstairs after you were done, avoiding any eye contact with him, as though you'd done something in his room that you were ashamed of. And now, to hope that he will remember you would sound too presumptuous. You revise: *Hi Kul, I'd come to your place last Sunday, um, to meet Pranav. I just wanted to know if he mentioned me in one of your conversations. Could you tell me how he felt about our date?* Crap! That's not how you begin a conversation with someone you're talking to for the first time. Instead, shouldn't you ask 'how are you or what's up?' and wait for his reply?

Oh God! What a freak he will think you are if he learns that you stalked his flatmate on social media. He's never going to talk to you. He will block you and ask his flatmate to block you too. How could this thought not have occurred to you before framing messages for him? Thank God you did not click the 'send' button. You shake off the idea, realizing how idiotic it would seem. Instead, you try to concentrate on your work again.

Thursday: March is not even fully over, yet it's getting uncomfortably warm with every passing day. You consider planning a trip to the hills with your friends. You float the idea on your college WhatsApp group amidst the trite 'good morning' messages and memes. There's no response initially. By 11 a.m., one of them responds, saying, 'Sounds like a good idea'. Your hopes are raised. But then the other says he is busy shopping for his upcoming wedding and can't afford to take leave; yet another friend says his work project is going live soon, so he has to stay back for it. Two of them are already married, the other one is getting married this year. In a year or two, all of them will be married and have their own families. Even the lone voice that had raised your hopes will go silent soon. Their limited off days from work will be spent with their wives and children while you are left to stalk the flatmates of failed dates.

But then the date went well, you correct yourself. Didn't it? After the make-out session, he went to fetch his bike, which was parked in the parking space of some random hotel after a drunken night out. It now occurs to you that he must have gone of there for one of those weird parties. How could you not have figured that out? That Sunday, you had asked to accompany him on the trip to fetch his bike. 'Oh, of course, I thought you may have other plans, so I didn't ask,' he'd said. You said you had to meet a friend for coffee, but you could do that a bit later. 'That's cool! Let's go then,' he had said, grinning at you.

Friday: You get into the shared cab with your hair half done. After sleeping late the previous night, you're late again. The way the other passengers look at you makes you uneasy. They hate you for keeping them waiting. The next person to board the cab is a young man who studies at one of the private universities close to your workplace. You've always found him annoying. You try to analyse why. It's his sense of entitlement that bothers you. He will ask for the AC to be turned on full blast. You were always taught that everything you get, or is vouchsafed to you, was the fruit of the benevolence of the divine; you could not claim anything.

This boy, on the other hand, thinks the world owes him a great deal. He is only twenty, for crying out loud. He orders a change of song on the FM if he doesn't like it. His banter with the cab driver, who's at least fifteen years his senior, borders on impertinence. And you still use your sorrys and thank yous, even though you've known the driver much longer. He plays music on his cell phone and assumes that everyone in the car would want to listen; he doesn't have the etiquette to ask if that's okay with everyone or should he put on his earphones? Today you are in no mood to entertain this nuisance. When it becomes unbearable, you shoot him a look of disdain and curtly ask him to use headphones. He looks shocked and the cab falls silent. You get back to your paperback. You can't concentrate, of course.

Your mind wanders back to your date with Pranav Bhalla: The two of you'd taken an auto to this random hotel. On your way, you had chatted about various things. He had confessed to feeling lonely when he comes back home. He had said he wants to have someone by his side when he wakes up. 'I sometimes call these silly boys over to stay the night so that I don't feel alone. But they don't like to cuddle and that's disappointing,' he'd added. You had expressed shock: how could someone not want to cuddle? Isn't it the best thing to do? You had wanted to ask if this was his oblique way of inviting you for an overnight stay. (Because if it was, you'd come gladly.) But you'd just nodded, lost in his deep, clear eyes. Secretly, you'd calculated the logistics in your head again.

Suddenly, your phone buzzes. It's Srinivas Ganeshan, a Tamil NRI from the US who is visiting his relatives. You've been talking to him for the past two months. You had met him while using Grindr on a date with someone else. Your date had run out for some errand, leaving you in the stinking room. You were bored, trying to come up with a polite excuse. You'd thought disappearing without a credible reason would be very rude. You'd opened Grindr, which is when you'd run into Srinivas. His charming sense of humour had made you laugh out loud, even when you were struggling to hold your breath and balancing your right hip on the edge of the bed which also stank.

Since then, you've been chatting over the phone regularly. But he doesn't have the eyes, dimples or the squeaky voice (which you'd first found odd, but now beautiful) of Pranav

Bhalla. He doesn't even have an American accent. He is a nice chap, though, and you enjoy talking to him. You take his call even if he calls at awkward hours. And he does that often. Sometimes you even wait for his calls, without telling him about it. He says silly things at times, you know, but you still find him endearing – he doesn't have any airs. He is not bothered by your condition. He had laughed it off. You had known that he would. He is not as intense, and maybe that's why he seems happier.

You take the call. His voice is comforting. He proposes visiting historical monuments and Sufi shrines in Delhi; he wants to explore the 'historical heritage of Delhi'. Only people freshly returned from the US would say things like that, you think. This is, it strikes you, what you find irritating in him. He is too ... too ... how would you put it ... 'cultured'? He makes a show of his fondness for Indian culture, which only people who are completely cut off from it can make. It's not fondness, it's nostalgia. Sanitized and convenient nostalgia, cleansed of all the heat, sweat, squalor, congestion that forms a part of the package deal called India. They don't want all of that; they just want to dress up in vibrant *dandia* costumes and dance to Falguni Pathak songs. You wonder why he doesn't realize its absurdity. You'd wanted to comment below his pictures of playing dandia on Facebook: 'But you never played dandia while you were in India. YOU'RE TAMIL, for Amma's sake!' instead, you'd written: 'Aw! You look so cute!'

He asks if you're still hung up on this guy. Is that why you're not coming? 'No, of course not. It's so hot. I will melt,' you say. 'You and your *nakhras*. If the sun could melt your fat, you would have readily come, I know.' He laughs. You laugh too, feebly.

Saturday: You're home with a long face. You haven't logged in to Grindr since your last date and don't feel the urge to. Porn doesn't titillate you. Your libido, like your self-confidence, has plummeted. Your mother notices that you've been behaving oddly for the past week. She asks if there's anything the matter with you. Is it work? Are you not happy with your new job?

You find this incredible and give her a look. You open your mouth to say something but then bury your head in the pillow again. She prods on, asking if there's too much work pressure. You feel like howling. You want to say that all your problems are not always about work. When have you ever been so visibly upset about work? You are not a machine meant only for earning money! You are a person with emotions and desires. You have a heart and you have a dick! Like other people your age you too want love and sex. Why doesn't she ever ask about your love life?

You'd even sent the guy a cat-meme last night, but he did not respond. You have been dumped! You want to howl and cry and break a few things, but you just say, 'I am tired, ma. Nothing is wrong. Just let me sleep. Shut the door when you go.' And off to sleep you go.

When you wake up, you decide to tackle that one problem that has plagued you all your life: your weight. You've never hated yourself for being gay, but you've always hated yourself for being overweight. You resolve to hit the gym for the third time in the last four years. You anticipate awkward questions from the trainer, surprised when, on your arrival, he asks none. He is used to it, you guess. You start working out, but your self-confidence has been pushed to the nether world. Your stamina has reduced, and you're panting before you've even begun exercising properly. You sit down to observe everyone around. You feel as if everyone is looking at you, thinking you're a failure. That's obviously untrue. In this temple of vanity, everyone is completely self-absorbed. No one has the time to look at you. You go into a meditative mood. You imagine the high priest of this temple telling you in a solemn voice: 'The more you lose, the more you'll gain; the more you gain, the more you'll lose.'

It occurs to you that the entire health and fitness industry is fuelled by lust. The groans and grunts of the men around you begin to unravel the masochistic appeal of this place: people inflicting pain of one kind upon themselves in the hope that they may escape another. Just when you begin to feel awful about yourself, you see an overweight girl struggling hard to bend forward. You want to go to her and tell her to stay put. You want to tell her that things will get better soon, that there's nothing she can't do. That her happiness does not depend on other people. So what if he doesn't care for you? Wait, that's what you want to tell yourself, not her, you realize, and you see the trainer (the high priest of the temple of vanity) looking at you with a stern face, and you start jumping again. He then points you to the stationary bike.

You recall, as you climb onto the bike, that Pranav had also asked you to climb his bike. You had initially replied, 'No, it's alright. I will just take a cab from here. I just wanted to hang out a bit with you. You go your way now.' Then he had given you a *don't-start-with-this-formality* look again and said, 'Please sit. Get a taste of my bike-riding skill too, *yaar*. I'd like it.' How could you have said no. You had climbed onto the pillion, wondering if it was alright to put your arms around his waist.

At the gym, a woman is lunging forward and backward about two feet away from you when one of her bra straps slips off her shoulder. She fixes it before anyone can notice. You pretend as though you haven't seen her. In turn, she pretends to ignore that you were checking out her husband who's assiduously doing his push-ups next to her. For a split second, a look passes between the two of you that says, *your secret is safe with me.*

The Way to Hell

My eight-year-old son Manu has a habit of eavesdropping on my phone conversations. Sometimes I wonder if his father has put him up to it. He is a sharp child, very observant and is growing up rather quickly. Lately, I've started waiting for him to fall asleep before discussing sensitive subjects with my husband. We've even started having sex in the drawing room. In fact, these days we have sex so rarely that the change of setting adds a sense of novelty.

Last night, when my brother Pranav called, Manu was listening intently, so I could not say much in response to Pranav's rant. Yes, Pranav was ranting. He said he had recently met a guy. At first, I thought he was sad because the date had gone badly, but I quickly learnt that was not the case, quite the opposite actually. He loved the guy. He was unsure if he wanted to take it further. Frankly, he and his ways don't make a lot of sense to me. I mean, I understand that he is different (and a bit difficult too) but why complicate life more than it already is. Whenever I say anything, he shuts me up by saying that I won't get it or that his world is very different than mine, ours.

Sometimes I am forced to think that his problem isn't that he's different, but that he's a bad judge of character. Today, he sounded as lost and sad as when he got entangled in the mess with his friend Rishabh. I had warned him at the time; I had always found Rishabh a little odd and too tall. Good-looking, but weird, though I had just seen a few pictures of him with Pranav. Sometimes you can tell these things from the appearance of a person, or even a picture.

My brother was so scared when Rishabh took his life. I remember it distinctly because Pranav was with me in Mumbai when it happened.

Pranav had just graduated and had moved to Hyderabad to look for work. He was sharing an apartment with Rishabh. In January 2009, when Manish and I went to Hyderabad to attend a wedding, Pranav came over to meet us. However, that night he asked if he could stay with us. At first, I thought he meant for just that night, so I said, 'Of course, you don't have to ask. The room is big enough.' But then he said he wanted to stay with us in Mumbai for a few days. It was unusual. Though he claimed to just want a change of scenery, I smelled a rat. I knew this sudden desire to move to Mumbai had to do with Rishabh. He looked a bit disturbed, so I did not prod further. I simply asked when we should expect him. He said he didn't want to go back to the flat – not even to pick up his belongings. The next day, we flew to Mumbai with my brother.

About a month later, Pranav's other friend, the heavy one, called to tell him that Rishabh had died by suicide in Hyderabad. Pranav was white as a sheet upon hearing the news and he remained in shock for about a month. He blamed himself for his friend's death. I tried to reassure him that it had nothing to do with him. Pranav had simply moved out of a city that could not offer him employment. Wallpapers and roommates change. They don't drive people to suicide.

Later, we found out that Rishabh was among the many people who had lost their employment due to the infamous collapse of Satyam Infotech, after a humongous accounting scam by its founder. I tried to convince Pranav that losing his job must have driven him to take such a dire step, not losing a roommate. But he was not willing to listen. He continued to blame himself.

This was, of course, when I did not know everything about Pranav's life. I mean, not everything about that aspect of it. But now that I do, I suspect that they were more than just friends. He barely talks about that episode now. He only says that he decided to move away from Rishabh to help him.

It's a really odd business, helping people. One never gets it right. To help people, sometimes you must remove them from your life, other times bring them closer. But it never goes as you planned. Like this girl, Nilu.

It has been almost a year now since Nilu came into our lives. She had suffered a lot of trauma at the hands of her father. I vividly remember the first time I met her. Their family had just moved from Bihar. Her large eyes caught my attention. When I asked her if she went to school, she burst out laughing, as if I'd cracked a joke. The very idea of receiving education and not selling vegetables at the age of nine sounded absurd to her. The echo of her laughter still rings in my head, disturbing me to the core.

My blood boils when I think about her father. Although I could have helped Nilu's mother file a case, she said that if I really wanted to help her, I should take Nilu with me. I had to take a call. It was an impulsive decision, I admit. Even so, I don't regret it. Both my father and Manish were against the idea. But I stood my ground. I had clearly told Manish the house was just as much mine as it was his. He relented in the end, though I could sense that he wasn't happy with my decision, and he didn't care to conceal it.

Things only got worse as he became preoccupied with his start-up. They had run into some legal trouble with the BMC – the municipal corporation. Manish would leave early in the morning and return late at night; even when he would come back, he would be busy with phone meetings, claiming he was trying hard to 'pull some strings.' He was also on the lookout for a manager, someone younger, more enterprising and, most importantly, trustworthy. Obviously, Pranav would have been the best choice; Manish even offered him equity, but it's difficult to convince Pranav to do anything that he doesn't want to. He is doing well in his field. Pranav had always wanted to be behind the camera. He is a creative person, not a businessperson. Why expect someone to do something they are not suited for? But I suppose Pranav is not new to such expectations; he's been battling them since he was a kid. Perhaps Pranav sensed that his refusal would please me more than it would upset my husband. Maybe 'please' is not the right word – I think it's 'relieve'. I felt *relieved* when Pranav turned down the proposal.

I didn't want the burden of justifying Pranav's choices to my husband every other day. Pranav is different, and Manish most definitely senses that. I am tired of fielding his crafty questions like, 'Shouldn't you find your brother a wife now?' or 'I am sure he has a girlfriend, no?' I already had a tough time explaining things to my parents. Papa still thinks that yoga and pranayam can fix my brother. Yes, my father believes that my brother needs *fixing.* He brings up this issue every time Pranav is back. I knew Pranav went to Jaipur only to escape Papa's snarky comments and unsolicited lectures. And I think that's the same reason he went to Hyderabad where he bunked with that wretched friend of his, and the same reason now he lives with that other friend of his, Kul Luthra, even though my parents have a big enough house in the same city. He says it's because of work. But we all know the truth. He wants to be away – away from these questions and taunts. And also, to sleep around with as many men as he wants.

I know Manish resents me for not being able to convince my brother to join his business venture in Mumbai. But I know it's for the better. For both of us.

Now, he also resents me for bringing Nilu along with me. Things were going fine till now. Nilu used to keep Manu company when both Manish and I were away at work. I don't wish to have a second child, but because Manu had no one to play with and felt lonely, I had started reconsidering the idea. However, with Nilu around, I did not have to worry about Manu's loneliness. She was getting along well with him. Manu found her odd at first, which was natural since she came from a very different background. But recently, he told me that he had taught her a few English words like 'sorry', 'thank you' and even the names of the seven days.

Manish kept accusing me of taking undue advantage of the girl, but I don't understand why. I've provided her a safe environment, a comfortable life and a friend; in return she helps with some domestic chores. How is that exploitation? I simply thought it would be better to provide her with a home than sending her to some NGO where I don't know if she will get personal care. But now, I'm afraid I'll have to look for such an NGO. Maybe I'll speak with my friend Poonam. I think her sister-in-law runs a shelter, or maybe she knows someone who does. Manish won't listen to me anymore.

I am worried about Manu, though. He's a sensitive boy. Sometimes I worry that he is too soft-hearted. The world is a mean place, not meant for those with tender hearts. Last year, we went out for dinner on Manish's birthday. As we stepped out of the restaurant, two street kids began trailing us, asking for money and food. We kept walking towards the parking area. Manu looked at them with a mix of wonder and sympathy. While Manish was reversing the car, one of the kids began to knock on the half-open window, blocking the rear-view mirror. Manish asked him to step away from the car as he rolled up the window. For a few seconds, the kids ran after our car till they could no longer keep pace. Manu was watching all this silently. Within minutes of starting, I fell asleep.

After reaching home, I asked him to change and check if he had packed his school bag for the next day. But he did not move. Since he is usually obedient, I was a bit surprised. I thought maybe he was tired. When I asked to help him pack his bag, he didn't say anything. I knew something was wrong. I bent down, cupped his face with my hands and asked again. As he looked at me with his teary, large eyes, his lower lip started to quiver and, within a second, he started crying hysterically. Manish rushed out of our bedroom and asked what had happened. I told him I had no clue. Both of us tried to console Manu for a few minutes before he said anything coherent. He then pointed at Manish and said, 'Papa is very bad!' Manish half-smiled. As the accused party, he could not cross-question Manu. I wiped Manu's tears with my dupatta and said, 'Papa will say sorry if you tell us what bad thing he has done.'

Controlling his sobs, he said, 'Papa did not give food to those kids and shut the window on them … they were hungry … and he—' Before he could complete, he broke down in tears again. I had to hug him. Manish tried to justify himself: 'Beta, I was reversing the car; he was blocking my view. There could have been an accident.' But nothing worked. He kept crying inconsolably and went on repeating, 'They were hungry, ma!'

Finally, we had to drive back to that place and find those kids. We ordered a meal and gave it to them. They called four more kids like them. And Manu asked us to feed them too. And so, we did. Manu watched all of them eat and smiled at us. He was happy in a way only children can be. I don't know when and how we lose that art.

Manish and I had the same conversation on our drive back, with Manu asleep in the back seat. I told him how Manu's extremely vulnerable side bothered me. He said that Manu's too young for me to be worried about anything. But Manu needs to understand we can't solve all the problems of the world. We can't feed every hungry child. Am I a bad mother if I shatter my child's idealism at such a young age and teach him pragmatism? Or am I a bad mother if I let him live in a fantasy land where he thinks he can save the world, only to learn the hard way that he can't? A disillusioned idealist often becomes a bitter revolutionary or a lousy philosopher. I'm not sure if I want my son to become either. I've come to realize the hard way that you can't help everyone. Look what mess I have made of my family.

I don't know what to do now. Some valuables and cash are missing from the house. So are both the kids. Manish is sitting at the breakfast table, yelling at me to fetch his gadgets and wallet. How do I tell him they are missing, along with Manu. My heart is sinking. I am feeling confused, angry and helpless all at once. What if they have run away? Could Nilu have convinced him to steal money and run away? My Manu never steps out of the house without asking me. Am I overthinking? Maybe they simply went downstairs to play. But I can see the lawn from here, and it's empty. Even if they went to play, why would they take the gadgets and wallet with them? O God, what if she is part of some kind of a crime syndicate? Was she planted here? If we report the matter to the police, they will ask why we did not get her verified earlier and how did she come to live with us in the first place? Keeping an unverified servant at home is against the RWA policy. They too will turn against us. But Nilu wasn't a servant. She just helped me with some domestic chores, nothing more.

Take Me for a Ride

... IT'S NICE TO have educated passengers like you, sir. Some customers are very difficult. Just because I am driving a cab does not mean you can take me for a ride. There was this woman who once tried to trick me into driving her daughter to the airport. She too had an early morning flight like you. Looks like you have an international flight, sir? Don't worry, sir, nobody misses their flight when they're in Chandar's cab. I also want to go abroad one day. I am no beginner, though I may look like one. I have seen enough of the world by now.

I have lived in three cities already. I was born in Jalandhar. Do you know Jalandhar, sir? It is in Punjab. After my mother eloped with her *yaar,* I lived with my father. I don't blame my mother. My father was a bastard. *Bhadwa,* we call him in my language. He used to sell undergarments for a living. My mother used to say that he could even sell his own underwear if he had no money to buy alcohol. Sometimes he would try to sell my mother too. One day, she ran away with a customer. She wasn't a bad woman, my mother. She left me behind because she knew I could look after myself. She is no more now. I learned of her death from my mausi, my mother's sister. But when she had disappeared, my father went mad with anger. He was so angry, he broke my head. Well, almost. You know how things are in this country: boys are punching bags and girls are doormats.

He kept me alive hoping she would come back for me and then he would exact his revenge. But she never returned. Not until the time I was there. I, too, being my mother's son, escaped soon and took a train to Mumbai. Such a filmy story, you might think.

I was probably eighteen when I reached Mumbai. Right after my class 12 examination. I slept on the railway platform for a while, then on footpaths. But I was my father's son after all. His salesman skills had rubbed off on me. No, I didn't sell underwear. My choice was more *sanskari*. I found work in a saree showroom. First my job was to open the showroom in the morning, clean it, light incense, put new sarees on display, and transport sacks and stacks of sarees from the godown to the showroom. The money was so little that it was almost a joke. But I knew I had to start somewhere. The owner spotted my talent and promoted me to sales within months. I still didn't have a place to stay. I used to sleep in the godown.

I had started doing sales but I retained my morning tasks. And one of them was to buy spare flowers and garlands for the gods at the showroom. That's how I met Malti. She used to sell flowers and garlands right outside the godown. Because she saw me coming out every morning, she asked me if I was looking for a place. I thought she was a godsent. She told me she can offer to keep me as a tenant for a small sum of money. When I asked her why was she being nice to me, she said I reminded her of her son who passed away. He was my age. There were three children left. The eldest was nine. They slept in the ascending order, between their parents. When I saw the tiny house, I asked Malti where I would sleep. Looking me up and down, she clicked her tongue vigorously. She stacked the kerosene stove and a few utensils lying in the corner of the tiny kholi and pointed me to the cleared area. That was my bedroom for at least eight months.

Her husband, too, like my father, was a drunkard. He did laundry at a hospital. Or that is what she told me. I never had a full conversation with him, because he used to leave before me and by the time he would return, he was too drunk to talk sensibly. Sometimes, when he saw me eating, he used to remark that I ate like their dead son. Malti would then ask him to shut up and sleep so they don't lose another tenant. That's me. I was their tenant. They spoke in Marathi. I could not fully understand what they said, but I could make sense of it from whatever broken Marathi I'd picked up from the children. For example, I'd learnt that food is called *jevan*. I am good at picking up languages. After the rent I paid, I was left with little money, just enough for a *vada-pav* twice a day. But Malti was kind. She sometimes gave me leftover curry rice from their dinner.

The month of July was the worst. It rained so heavily, all the rainwater seeped through the cracks and collected in my corner on the uneven floor. The sleeping order was changed according to which I had to sleep next to Malti. When it rained, it seemed like the kholi would collapse at any moment under the heavy downpour, but Malti would say her kholi was blessed by Sai Baba; not even Indra, the god of rain, could harm it. And she was right, except for the waterlogging and seepage, nothing happened to the kholi.

On one such rainy night, kept awake by an angry army of mosquitoes, I tossed around on my tattered mattress. The kholi was mean and suffocating, reeking mildly of urine and fart. Other than the light creeping in from under the door, it was completely dark. I suddenly felt a hand on my crotch. For a moment I stayed still, thinking it could have been an accident. After all, we were all crammed together. But it did not stop. From the softness of the touch, I knew it was Malti's hand. Had she mistaken me for her husband? I was struggling to remain indifferent, which she sensed. She was now feeling the full growth with her hands as if she had been asked to report on its length and girth in a medical report. I don't like to brag. Let me just say, if she were to write a report, nothing in it could embarrass me – everything would be *above average*. But I would be surprised if she could spell her name on paper without mistakes, never mind writing detailed reports.

I squirmed. Okay, I agree, I had eyed her full breasts a few times, but that's because it's difficult not to notice them. If you see them, you will realize. That doesn't mean I thought of her this way. But there she was: fondling me eagerly. When I sat upright to see what was going on, she pulled me back with the other hand to get me to keep quiet. She slid her hand under my pyjama and placed her right leg on me. In whispers, I asked her what she was doing. She shushed me by placing a finger on my mouth. When I asked about Bala *bhau,* I heard her giggle softly. She then said he wouldn't wake up even if elephants were to trumpet in his ears, so drunk he was. *'Bolu nakos. Chala maja karu ya,'* she whispered. Don't talk. Let's just have some fun.

I have always looked mature for my age and have always been well built. Earlier I used to play a lot of cricket and work out at a local gym. I have been this tall since I was fourteen, so there's no way she could have guessed my real age. I didn't want to tell her it was my first time. My nervousness was hidden by the darkness, Malti's heaving and Bala bhau's loud snores. In the dank atmosphere of that small kholi, the mushrooms of illicit intimacy were bound to grow. After we were done, she quietly rolled over and dozed off. I was left to relish my first experience of being a man and, of course, to fight the mosquitoes.

After that, it almost became routine. Every other night, within half an hour of the lights going off, she would slide over and I would feel Malti's hand tugging at my pants. I will admit, sometimes I took the lead too. You wouldn't want to sleep next to Malti if you were me, but believe me, you wouldn't regret a night with her.

A year on, I started driving a tempo in Mumbai. Malti's cousin was a tempo distributor, who was looking to hire. I pounced at the opportunity. Since then, I have been driving.

I moved to Delhi four years back. My mausi lives here. I have my own car now. I mean it belongs to my mausi but she can't drive it. Her husband, my *mausa,* died last year. And they have two daughters. One of them is married. The other one yet to be married. A part of my salary goes to her wedding fund. Delhi is not bad. But I miss Mumbai. I miss Malti whenever it's dark and raining. I had sex with many girls after her, but none as skilful as Malti.

My friends run to G. B. Road or bring the girls home. Once they brought a girl to my place when Mausi had gone to Haridwar. But I didn't even touch the girl. Don't you believe me? I am serious. Okay, I asked her to suck me, but nothing more. I never do these girls. They are no fun. They don't know how to pleasure me. Except for Shabina.

Shabina is my dream girl. My friend Harish, a quiet one, brought her to his place once. He tried to keep it secret, but he couldn't. *Saala chhupa rustam nikla*! Our friend Mukesh told Anwar and me about his secret pleasures, and the three of us showed up at his place. On the way, I asked Mukesh the reason Harish had to bring a whore; his wife is so pretty. Mukesh said he has been fucking Shabina for two weeks now and when I'd see Shabina, I'd understand why. And he wasn't wrong. When I saw her the first time, I couldn't form a proper sentence, all I could say was, '*Abey ... bhenchod!*'. Sir, don't mind, please. I get carried away sometimes.

Shabina can replace any Bollywood heroine. Never seen a prettier girl in my life. I am telling you, sir, you will easily forget Katrina Kaif if you see Shabina. Smooth, slim, sexy – she was everything you'd want in a woman. Only, she wasn't a woman. Number six, do you understand? But, by God, you wouldn't ever be able to tell if you just saw her on the street. It's only when she spread her legs that you realized that she was a little different than others. But she really wasn't. She was more feminine than most other girls I had seen. Her voice too was like a bell of silver. I have never enjoyed fucking a woman this much. Her tongue can work magic on you. She had made me crazy. After that day, I had become addicted to Shabina. I had started calling her at least twice a week at Harish's place. Mausi had come back from Haridwar, you see. Harish and Anwar too could not get enough of her. The best part was she did not have nakhras like other whores. You could do anything with her. Just anything, you know! She also talked so well. Other whores don't know a thing about talking to customers. Only filth rolls off their tongue. You just have to cover their face and fuck the base. But not Shabbo (that's what I had started calling her). Her tongue was dipped in honey. If she were a regular woman, we wouldn't have been able to afford her in this lifetime. So, we were thankful that God had made her different.

Shabbo is not an ordinary woman. Yes, sir, for me she is a woman and will always be. What I mean is, she is educated. She is doing a correspondence course from the Delhi University. It's funny you still haven't asked me how I can speak in English so well. Almost all my customers ask the same question. But I'll tell you anyway. Shabbo taught me. She went to an English-medium school, you see. And now she is doing BA in English. She sometimes reads thick books. I ask her what's the use of these books when she has to suck cocks at night. She says reading books feeds her mind, and sucking cocks feeds her stomach; both are important. Sometimes she says such fundoo things that blow my mind. Who knows if she steals them from the books she reads. But I couldn't care less. We started spending a lot of time together. In about a year she taught me how to use the language. Use it well, I mean. I knew the basics. I used to own an English-to-Hindi dictionary earlier. Shabbo called it trash and said she would get me a new one. Look, sir, I am not one of those cheap men who accept gifts or money from whores. I know of many such guys who even live off the earnings of their so-called girlfriends from the red-light area. I am not one of those. If it was something other than a book, I wouldn't have even touched it. But I was confused when she gave it to me. There were no word meanings in it. When I asked her what she had bought, she then pointed to the English words. I asked her again where the fuck were the meanings. The thing is, until then, I thought word meanings meant Hindi. Shabbo gave me a puzzled look. I was irritated, so I called her a dumb whore. If a person understood English words, then why would he even need the dictionary. I explained to her how stupid it was to buy a dictionary only in English. She laughed and patted my head. I told her, in strict words, to never laugh at me. Shabbo was everything I'd been warned against. She was a whore, and to top it, she could read. *Harrafa*! Do you know, sir, the word 'Harrafa' which is used as an insult, actually comes from the word '*Harf*' meaning 'letters that make up words? Funny it's used for a prostitute, while it actually means a woman who can read and write. Women are cunning. And if they are educated, then only God save you from them. But I can't forget how pure her laughter was, how beautiful she looked when she laughed.

One night when Harish was out on duty and I was at his place, I called Shabbo. I called up Anwar to ask him if he wants to come, but he said his son is sick. I don't know why I felt happy knowing that Shabbo would only spend time with me. She came an hour late, wearing a pale expression and a shining sari. I wanted to take her to task for turning up late, but when she smiled at me, my anger vanished. She switched off the lights and started taking off her clothes within minutes. She was always in hurry, I had noticed. I asked her if she wanted water or alcohol. She said no. Then she stopped undressing midway. She asked if she could lie down for a while before we started. This was unusual, but I agreed. I sat next to her with her head in my lap. When I asked her what was wrong, she did not say anything. Seeing her beautiful body, I couldn't resist. She must have felt my erection. She tried to move but I pinned her and unzipped my pants. I thrust her head down and she started doing her job. I removed whatever clothes were left on her body. She had transported me to heaven. I was very close to climaxing when I spanked her, but she howled and shrunk back. I was stunned because she had never behaved this way. I was furious because the rhythm was broken. '*Randi ... madarchod*!' I burst out. She started whimpering. I felt guilty but did not know why. She was a whore. I had spanked her many times in the past. I hitched up my underwear and asked her what was the matter. She stayed silent. I switched on the light. Now I could see bruises on her body. She started crying. I told her to either tell me what was the matter or leave my room. Of course I did not want her to go, but I had to sound rough otherwise she wouldn't have stopped crying. Scared to be thrown out, she told me everything. Three policemen had told her the new SHO doesn't allow whoring business. When she said she had paid her due for the month to the previous SHO and refused to move until the following month, they beat her up and raped her. They were drunk, she said.

I would not have believed her, if it were not for her bruises. There was one thing that my useless father had taught me: never trust whores and politicians. But I knew she wasn't lying. They had hit her badly. She is so delicate, my Shabbo; even when I gently spank her, her fair skin turns *sindoor* red for hours. They can't be real men, three of them beating her together!

Of course, I made her a drink. I did not know how else to comfort her. Booze is the best medicine for all wounds. Hers is a sad story, sir. You know, I feel really bad for her. That night she talked to me about her past for the first time. She comes from an upper-caste Thakur family in Nepal. Her family tried hard to hide the fact that Shabbo was not like her other siblings, but not for too long. She loved wearing make-up and dressing up. Her father had warned her against it many times. Once when she was about fifteen, he caught her secretly applying a flaming red lipstick in front of the bathroom mirror. He thrashed her so badly that she had broken limbs. That was the day she decided to run away. She came to Delhi with a lover, who pimped her out and started using her money. She dumped him and started saving money for herself. When I asked for her real name, she said Shabina was who she was, and there was no other name that she'd like to remember or be remembered by.

Despite her protests that night, I took her to the nearest government hospital. I hate going to hospitals; people pay so much money to just die there – it's ridiculous. The emergency ward of a government hospital is the worst of all. There is never enough room. There were patients piled up on top of each other on some beds, and some lay squeezed side by side on stretchers. At first I didn't know what to do and whom to talk to. For a moment I regretted taking Shabbo there. Until now, she was only bruised. She would get to know that I don't know anything about hospitals. I thought she will laugh at me. But I saw her speaking to a woman who was wiping the floor. The woman directed us to a counter. I scolded Shabbo for talking to people without my permission.

Behind the desk were two young men and a woman. The woman was scribbling something in a register. The men in white doctor coats were watching something on their phones. One looked up and asked in a tired voice what the case was. I did not know what to say. The case was: the whore I fuck had been beaten and raped by few policemen. It sounded strange. But what could these doctor do about it? Shabbo came forward and said that she had hurt herself from a fall. The woman stopped writing in the register and looked up. Shabbo said that her wounds needed dressing, that's all. The woman eyed me with suspicion. She asked me how we were related. I stayed silent for a second before asking if there was a senior doctor around. Staring at me with weird eyes, the woman handed me a form. She asked me if I knew how to read and write. Bitch! I quietly took the form and started filling it out. I asked Shabbo what's her last name and her age. I realized Shabbo was four years my senior. I was stuck at Gender. There were only two boxes. The lady doctor was watching us constantly. I hated that woman. I wanted to bang her head against the desk. I hated myself for bringing Shabbo to the hospital. I hated that she was stuck in this mess. I hated her for getting raped. I hated her for being a whore. But I most hated her for not being a woman. A proper woman.

Shabbo asked me to leave that part blank. The lady doctor pointed to a bench and asked her to wait there. Then the woman whispered something in the ears of the other two doctors. One of them called me aside. He asked me again, in a sterner voice this time, about Shabbo. He asked me what was the *bhasad* all about? Do you know what bhasad means? Like, fuss. He said she wouldn't be treated until we showed them a copy of the FIR. The other doctor walked up to us. 'You see what we have to deal with here,' he said, pointing to a patient with multiple stabs, his clothes soaked in blood. Wanting to puke, I said she'd been raped and that we wanted a medical test. 'People like you come here and waste our time. If whores and eunuchs also started complaining of rape then we won't find time even to breathe,' the young doctor said before he moved towards the man covered in blood. I was so angry. I didn't know whether it was frustration or embarrassment or both. The other doctor standing next to me said, '*Oye* hero, show your anger to your wife at home. Nothing good will come out of it here. Go file an FIR, then come back.' He too left. The lady doctor, seated behind the desk, was watching us, but as soon as I looked at her, she went to back to doing something in her register.

Shabbo was sitting on the bench, maybe waiting for a signal from me. Her eyes said, *let's go from this place.* The lady doctor looked at Shabbo and smirked. I swear on my mother, I wanted to bang her head with the thick register she was writing in.

Anyway, I went up to Shabbo and told her that we have to file an FIR. She just shook her head vigorously, saying I had gone mad. How could I even imagine that the police act against their own, she asked. 'Don't be stupid, Chandar. They will book us both under 377 and lock us up, only to fuck me once again and thrash you black and blue,' she said. I knew she was right. I knew that the police in Delhi were brutal. But then I couldn't have admitted that she was right. Just when I was about to yell at her, she started sobbing. I could see the bruises on her neck. So I couldn't say anything. I asked her to sit.

Both Shabbo and I sat on the bench for a few minutes, not sure what to do. On the bed opposite us, there was a tiny old man. Dark and defeated. He was paralysed. His lower lip was drooping with some spit hanging from the side. I could see he was lying there waiting for death, not treatment. I told you, sir, most people are taken to hospitals not to be kept alive, but so that they may die with dignity ... so that they may die on the hospital staff's watch. We take people to hospitals because we don't want to be burdened with guilt. I could have sat there the whole day watching that small old man with jammed limbs and droopy lips, but the strong odour of phenyl distracted me. The woman who had pointed us to the help desk was still mopping the floor. She stood next to us and asked to raise our feet so that she could mop the floor under the bench. She was studying us closely. The bite mark on Shabbo's neck drew her attention. Shabbo covered it up with her dupatta and asked me to move along. The woman stopped us. She patted Shabbo's shoulder gently and then went up to the lady doctor behind the counter, pointing at us.

The doctor suddenly got up from her chair and gestured Shabbo to come to the desk. Shabbo looked at me for approval. We both made our way towards her, but the doctor asked me to go back, saying she could handle Shabbo alone. In reply, I said, 'I am not going anywhere. You tell me what you want from my woman.'

Now, all three women were staring at me. The doctor asked if Shabbo was my wife. I said, 'What if she is not yet, she will be soon.' Shabbo swore at this and told me I had gone crazy. It was clear she was angry. I never understand these women. You can never tell what they think. Shabbo was just like any other woman in such matters. I don't even know why God decided to make her different. But I wasn't going to stand there listening to a whore swearing at me. I also gave it back to her. The lady doctor, silencing us both, threatened to get us thrown out if we raised our voices. I told her straightforwardly, 'Look, madam, we have no interest in being here. My woman has been assaulted by policemen. I just want you to confirm it.' She first yelled at a nurse who had just returned from her tea-break. The nurse yelled back at the doctor, saying that she was already working overtime, because another woman was on leave. Tired, the doctor turned to me again and said, 'You, hero, listen to me carefully. I can't conduct any test on your woman. You heard what the other two said. This is a police case. File an FIR. If you want, I can dress her wounds but that's all. Send her in or I will ask the guard to throw you out right now.'

The woman who was mopping the floor said to Shabbo, 'Don't be a fool. Men are hot-headed. Don't listen to him. Get your wounds dressed. Today he is with you, tomorrow he will forget you and bring another one. Don't try to mess with the police. We see such cases every day.' Shabbo released her hand from my grip and went behind the makeshift curtain, followed by the lady doctor.

Since that day I have always hated the police of this city. They are rascals; they will take away your money and your dignity. They will first grab your collar, then talk. They will take advantage of you if they know you are helpless. They will heckle whores and eunuchs or young boys who visibly don't belong here. It's crazy here. You need to be raised in Delhi to be able to deal with the cops here. The cops in Mumbai were different. The best thing about driving in Mumbai is the cops there. All of them are very polite. They might take money but they will never disrespect you. I will give you a simple mantra if you want to drive without getting into trouble in Mumbai. Actually, why should I lie. I don't like to take undue credit. This mantra was given to me by my boss in Mumbai, Malti's cousin.

The mantra is: just keep going, don't stop, don't block the flow at any point, just keep going, don't care for the rules as long as you keep going. All the rules apply to you only when you stop. Once you've been pulled up, just fold your hands and shell out the money that you can. You will never get in trouble. I have tried it myself, it works. *Arey*, but some people take it to a different level only. Take the latest hit-and-run case from Mumbai, for instance. Did you read about it? It's everywhere in the news and on Facebook. A car ran over two little kids. Their pictures were there on the front page. A boy and a girl. They were apparently running away. They had some cash and an iPhone on them. There were pictures of both the children. I can't get the large eyes of the girl out of my head. One of the kids died on the spot but the other survived, the reports said. The bastard didn't stop to even look back.

I always drive safely. You must have seen I did not jump any red light though the roads were empty, and you have a flight to catch. I like your name, sir. Srinivas Ganeshan. Very impressive. I like South Indians. Do you understand any Hindi? Now they want everyone to learn Hindi. I think it's unfair. See, I hardly used any Hindi with you. I know my customers. I care for them. I never turn down customers. Once you are out on the road to work, you can't have hang-ups. I learned this mantra from Shabbo. She also wants to make it big one day. Sometimes I have to remind her that I drive a cab and she gets fucked for a living. But whenever I feel lost, she brings me back on track. She says the best thing about the present is that it is not permanent. Let me tell you, sir, I also drove that woman's daughter, and her son-in-law too. But I told them, 'You will have to book a ride on the app. I won't take you just like that.' You can see why I have such a high rating. The passenger is our god. I hope you will also give me five stars, sir.

For international departures, we have to take a right turn from here; just two more minutes and we will reach. Please don't mind, I talk a lot. It helps me stay awake in the wee hours. How much music can one listen to, after all. I am so sorry, sir, I have been going on and on; I even forgot the question you asked that got me started.

Srinivas looked up from his phone. 'Um, as I recall, I'd just asked, "How are you?"'

Inconvenience is Regretted

ANGAI HUGGED SAMAR lightly. 'So precious you have become. I get to see you only once a year.'

'Has it really been that long?' Samar asked. They were sitting in the same coffee shop where their paths had crossed earlier.

'Yes, I think it was sometime in late December – can't remember the date now – when we ...' Angai paused. Then, after a moment of hesitation, he added, 'you know ... I had come over to your place. And it was about a week before that when we met here.'

Angai's guess was not far off. Save for a brief interlude at Samar's office in January that year. Angai's cell phone had needed repair, so he had called Samar before dropping it off at the service centre, conveniently close to Samar's workplace.

'Listen, the technician here says that it'll take at least three hours to fix the phone. I don't want to go back home and come all the way again to pick it up. Do you mind if I come over? If you're not too busy, of course. I just want to kill these three hours.'

There was a long silence at the other end before Samar spoke in his smooth, polished teakwood-desk voice, 'Of course. Come over. I have work, but you can sit by my side and watch me work.'

'I just didn't know what else to do at this odd hour in the middle of the day, so I thought of calling you. I have a book. I'll sit and read, and try not to bother you,' Angai said in a rush to dispel any awkwardness.

'We'll figure something out. Come on over! It's very cold outside,' Samar insisted.

The receptionist asked Angai to wait, pointing at a couch. 'I will inform sir,' she said picking up the receiver.

After a few minutes, Samar appeared on the scene. 'Hi Angai, come this way,' he said stiffly.

While the receptionist's bony fingers swiftly typed on the keyboard, her mascara-laden eyes were fixed on Angai. She seemed slightly startled, as if caught off guard, when Angai smiled at her before following Samar into the elevator. She returned a well-rehearsed smile.

'Press 4,' Samar instructed, as the elevator doors closed. 'You look like a tomato in this sweater, you know.' He pulled Angai's cheek, sounding like his normal self again.

'This wasn't planned,' Angai said. 'I would have chosen my attire more carefully if I had known I'd land up at your workplace.'

'Really?' Samar stretched the word playfully, as though accusing Angai of fabricating. 'Just admit that you wanted to see me,' he teased before they stepped out of the elevator.

The passage from the elevator to Samar's room wasn't too wide. Along the corridor were framed photographs of large buildings and complexes – some completed, others under construction, scaffolded and surrounded by massive equipment that Angai recognized but couldn't name. Samar was playing his part as the Project Manager at a semi-private construction company perfectly. Angai felt out of place, even intrusive, as he saw people smiling at Samar while passing him by, receiving approving nods in return. He suddenly became conscious of his flaming red sweater that made him stand out in an otherwise subdued space. He should not have just landed at Samar's workplace like this, unprepared, uninvited. But it was too late to turn back. As they reached the end of the long lobby, its polished floor gleaming under the lights fixed across the ceiling, Samar pointed to the room where they were to sit.

'So, I'll be in this conference room today. I just had my laptop and other stuff moved here. It somehow feels warmer; plus, it is mostly vacant,' Samar explained as the door shut behind him. 'Come, come … make yourself comfortable.'

They sat across each other, with a large conference table between them. 'Do you mind if I finish this?' Samar asked, opening his laptop.

'Of course not. Please, carry on. I told you I have a book to read.'

Samar rang for tea and went back to working; while Angai took out his copy of *Persuasion* from his bag and tried to concentrate on it. He had imagined that Samar would make some excuse – after all, the workplace is supposed to be a guarded space, insulated from any 'deviant' practices. Inviting a visibly effeminate man with whom one had slept a month ago could pose a risk of exposing oneself to gossip at best and scandal at worst. But Samar had surprised him.

Was it recklessness or genuine affection, Angai could not decipher.

Through the next two hours, they chatted sporadically. Angai wondered if he should ask whether he did the right thing by coming over. But fearing the answer, he instead asked mundane questions about the current project Samar was overseeing.

Samar did not say anything for about two minutes, as though he had not registered the question. He was focused on the laptop screen, his brows furrowed and the tip of his tongue sneaking out from the corner of his mouth – an action that made Angai tingle with desire. With a dramatic tap on the keyboard, Samar finally looked up. 'I don't supervise just one project. I'm not that lucky. I currently have three on my hands.' He leaned back in his chair and ran his hand over the back of his neck. 'In fact, the new one is in Bangalore, which means I'll have to travel more.' He sighed.

'I guess I should get going,' Angai said, getting up and gathering his things. 'I am sure they must have fixed it by now,'

'So soon? *Kyu*? There's no hurry on my end.'

'I know, and I must thank you for letting me come over. I really appreciate this. But I should leave now.'

'Why are you like this?' Samar frowned. 'Stop sounding like characters from your Jane Austen novels,' he said, standing up. 'I'll walk you out but come here before you go.'

There was a small doorway right behind Samar's chair. It led to another grand room adjacent to the conference room.

'What's going on?' Angai asked as he followed Samar into the other room.

'Just come, *baba*!'

Angai observed the plush interiors of the room, furnished with leather couches, a bulky writing desk, an LCD and potted palms.

'So this is my boss's room. He uses it when he's around. And because he is not here, I thought we might use it for a while, if you know what I mean,' Samar said, winking.

Without waiting for Angai's response, Samar grabbed him by the collar and kissed him. Angai clutched Samar's hand and whispered, 'Are you crazy? What if there are cameras around?'

Samar stepped back to survey the room. He then studied Angai's mouth which was now flushed to match the red of his sweater. It was impossible to resist. He grew hard. He pushed Angai against the wall, and let Angai unzip him.

'Let me know when you reach home, okay?' Samar said later, walking with Angai to the elevator.

'I'll go from here. Don't bother. Um ... when do I see you next?'

'Soon, I hope,' Samar replied.

In the eleven months that rolled by, they made plans to meet 'casually'. But none that materialized. And neither of them pushed too hard. They were neither lovers, nor friends. Both knew it was unlikely they would become either. Yet, they tried having a little fun down the road to oblivion. Occasionally, Angai would allude to Samar in a poem on his blog. Sometimes Samar would send a message when passing by the coffee shop where they first met. But without the promise of a future to fuel them, the perfunctory planning too gradually stopped.

Soon, the WhatsApp messages stopped as well. Once in a while, on his way back home from work, Samar would call Angai partly out of boredom, partly out of fondness. When they ran out of subjects to talk about, Angai would listen to the songs Samar hummed along with the radio or to the salvo of swear words Samar launched when someone overtook him from the wrong side. Class and crass coexisted in Samar – like in Delhi – just minutes away from each other, and it amused Angai to see him flit between the two with a natural ease. A slight push or provocation was all it took to bring about the change.

During one such phone call, when there was nothing else to fill the silence, Angai asked if Samar's search for a match had yielded any positive result. 'I don't know why, but things don't work out somehow. I am beginning to get tired of it now,' he said. Angai thought for a moment and slyly remarked, 'You are way past the marriageable age – what other choice do you have but to marry me!' They laughed, bound by an unburdened affection.

Both of them went on with their lives, hoping, groping, desiring – and retiring every now and then. Months passed before they spoke again.

Angai was at his cubicle when he received a call from Samar. He had not seen that name flash on the phone screen for a while. The same mix of excitement and inertia from their first call gripped him. The phone buzzed in his hands as he marched out.

'Hi … Long time!' he squeaked. 'How have you been?'

Samar returned with 'Hello.'

'I thought you had gone to hide in some Himalayan cave,' Angai joked.

'Very funny. How are you?'

'What do you want to hear? Let me humour you today.'

'Why did it take you so long to answer the call?'

'I was walking to the lounge for privacy.'

'*Nikla nahi abhi tak*? Isn't it time for you to leave?' Samar asked.

'I was just wrapping up. What's wrong? You sound low.'

'No, I just wanted to talk. I was feeling a bit … a bit—' he fell silent for a few seconds, before adding, 'Do you know where I'm calling from?'

'I have no clue. I hope you're not driving. I keep telling you it's risky.'

'I'm at the same coffee shop where we met … in fact, in the same corner.'

Angai sensed the dip in Samar's pitch. He pictured the upper story of the coffee shop in his head, imagining Samar, formally dressed, sitting next to the glass wall.

'You are? You could have asked me to join you. I could do with some coffee right now.'

'I know. I feel silly for not asking you before. I should have called you. I left work early today. God, I should have …'

'That's okay. We can meet some other time,' Angai said.

'No, I want to meet you as soon as possible.'

'Will you tell me what the fuck is the matter?'

After a minute of silence, Samar spoke. 'I've met a girl. We're getting married in a month or so.'

Angai fumbled. 'Oh, well, congratulations! When and where did you guys meet?'

'Our families arranged everything. I'm not super excited about it. It's a sinking feeling, Angai.'

'Are you second-guessing your decision?'

'I don't know. I've become emotionally numb. Nothing affects me. For me, it's a rite of passage maybe.'

'But you knew this would happen sometime, didn't you? So why do you feel like this?' Angai's question was aimed more at himself than at Samar.

'Didn't you hear? I said I just don't feel anything. Of course, I knew this would happen. I've been looking for prospects. But it feels weird when it actually happens. I guess I've gotten so used to having my personal space that I can't tolerate the idea of someone intruding on it. Not at this age now. It's too late to change ...' Samar went quiet. Then, as if seized by a sudden epiphany, he added, 'You know, if you want to get married, I suggest doing it early.'

Angai was overcome with a sense of *déjà-vu*. He was reminded of a Facebook post on the 'Humans of Delhi' page the previous week. Moved by it, he had shared the post on his wall. He made a mental note to read it again.

'Say something? Are you even listening?' Samar attempted to bring Angai's attention back to their conversation.

'Sorry. I was just thinking about ... never mind. Go on. I am listening.'

'I don't know what to say except that we're both doing it for our respective parents. We are both sailing in the same boat, in that sense. Her father is not keeping well, so she's eager to get this business over and done with soon – as some sort of a last wish, you know. We are both tired of looking further and might as well make do with whatever is at hand. She's a strong, opinionated woman who has been working and living by herself for a long time. She is probably as headstrong as I am, so I am not sure how this will work out,' Samar said.

'I think you're being too cynical, Samar. You can make this work. You just have to set aside your male ego, and I don't see any reason why you shouldn't. I'm sure she's also going to make compromises.'

'I know. We're both *compromising*, if that's the word you want to use. You should see my mother, though. I've never seen her more excited. I am going through with this for her. I'll be a good husband, I know that. Mechanically, I will do everything expected from me well. But I know I'll play a role.' Samar paused for a moment before adding, 'Will you see me again? I know how you feel about the whole thing.'

'Of course I will. Why wouldn't I?' Angai said hastily.

'I read your blog, you know. I read the one in which you criticized gay men for marrying women.'

'You did!' Angai exclaimed. He hadn't expected Samar to have the patience to read his prolonged posts.

'But you're not gay, Samar. You have a choice. I wrote about men who have no interest in women whatsoever,' Angai said, trying to sound sincere.

'Yeah, it is what it is. I'm not entirely off the hook, and I understand that. But I don't know any better. I'm not an activist like you. I don't meet as many people from the community. Apart from you, there is only one other guy I keep in touch with. You're the only person I've shared all these personal details with. And I am not sure if I'd stop talking to you even after I'm married.'

'Don't make this about us. It's about you.' Angai's voice hardened.

'No, I am serious, Angai. You know, whenever I read your posts on the blog, I searched for myself in them. It's crazy, but I did.'

'Well, you were there in several of them, Samar. Maybe you didn't read them carefully. That's not the point, though. You must give your best to this new endeavour and try to be as sincere as you can. Be fair to her, that's all.'

'Tell me you will see me tomorrow. I want to meet you before the year ends,' Samar said.

'I'll see if I can leave from work early tomorrow. But I can't promise.'

'Thanks for tonight. I was very low. It felt good to let out my feelings.'

'I'll always lend an ear. I won't judge you.'

'Come on! Of course, you will judge me, it's your passion,' Samar said.

'Well, honestly, if it were someone else in your place, I would. But it's you.'

'Why? Why would you go easy on me?'

'Good night, Samar. Let's see if we can meet tomorrow.'

'It's funny you still call me "Samar" even after all this while.'

'It's just easier. I am used to it now. That's also how I have stored your number in my phone,' Angai said. 'You take care.'

Angai straightened his clothes before entering the coffee shop. His eyes searched for Samar.

His phone buzzed. *'Exit frm gate no 2. M sitting upstairs. Same corner,'* the WhatsApp message said.

Angai climbed the stairs, his pace measured to feign nonchalance. He saw Samar, suave and smiling, rising from the couch, extending his hand to be shaken, ready to draw out and twist his vowels in his smooth voice. A flesh-and-blood person, not merely a romanticized figure in Angai's late-night blog posts. There he was, waiting to be heard, blamed and possibly, even vindicated.

'Wow, you look ... you look amazing, Angai! What have you been up to? God, just turn around. Have you been working out?'

'Stop teasing me!' Angai hugged Samar lightly. 'So precious you have become. I get to see you only once a year.'

'The loss is all mine, for sure,' Samar said, sinking into the couch. 'Has it actually been that long though?'

'Yes, I guess it was sometime in late December – can't remember the date now – when we ...' Angai paused and added after a moment of hesitation, 'you know ... I'd come over to your place. And it was about a week before that when we met here.' Even though he did not say it, he remembered the exact date: 29 December.

Angai was nervous, Samar could tell. Taking hold of Angai's hands, he gave them a squeeze.

'Your hands still get sweaty when you're excited.'

Angai only smiled in response. Samar stood up to check if the overhead AC near their couch was working.

'In kutton ko maine bola tha ye AC chala do. These idiots have not turned on the AC. It's stuffy in here,' he said, waving his hands in front of the wings of the machine.

Angai laughed inwardly. 'You're still as crass.'

'I know. Do you mind if I take off this coat and sweater? I'm sweating. I walked all the way here from my office.' Without waiting for Angai's reply, Samar removed his coat and sweater, and placed the moist sweater on Angai's lap.

Angai let out a 'Yuck!' while Samar grinned.

He then brought out his phone from his pocket and opened the picture gallery. 'Look at this. This was taken when I went to Bangalore last month. My friend and I were totally drunk in this picture. Don't we look it?' Samar said and swiped through the screen. 'And see this one taken in—'

Angai was distracted. Though he was nodding and hmm-ing dutifully, pretending to pay attention, he secretly appraised Samar from the corner of his eye. He felt an urge to run his hand through Samar's perfectly combed hair, anything to bring some chaos in life of this orderly man. 'Samar, who is this other guy you talked about yesterday?' he interjected.

Samar put the phone on the table. He called the waitress and asked her to switch off the overhead light. 'It's too bright, isn't it?'

'Answer the question,' Angai pressed.

'A charming boy studying in Australia. I met him at a bar in Sydney when I was there the year before the last. He is about to finish his course. Says he will move back to India soon. Emotional fool. We mostly chat over the phone. He says he really likes me and sends me these cute audio messages. No one has ever done that. I found it very cute,' Samar said.

'Oh, so he's Indian!' Angai's eyes narrowed. 'I'd never do that. Recording messages and all. Rather desperate,' he said curtly and picked up the menu.

Samar noticed Angai's lips. They shone with resentment. 'Have you used lip gloss? Like, a lot of it?'

'It's cold here, lips get chapped. This is not Sydney,' Angai retorted, without looking up from the menu in his hands. It was ironic that he should feel jealous of a boy vying for Samar's attention, given Samar's confession last night about his plans to marry a woman. But Angai did not resent her one bit. If anything, he sympathized with her.

'Stop staring at the menu and talk to me. I have already placed the order,' Samar said. When he did not get a response, he looked around and leaned in to softly kiss Angai's cheek. 'You are my favourite, dodo. I chased you. You and your nakhras. *'I don't wish to share my number,'* remember?' They both chuckled, sitting on opposite shores, tickled by the ripples of reminiscence.

Angai watched the young waitress carefully set down the cups on the table, almost apologetic for interrupting their conversation. He smiled at her, as though to say *it's okay.* Once she left, he asked, 'Did anyone else make it to your bed?'

'No. No one did. I swear on myself. No one else did. It was only you,' Samar said. 'I would never invite anyone into my home. I don't know what came over me in our case ...'

'Do you regret it?'

'Don't be silly. I had planned it properly. I was in Meerut with my folks at my aunt's house. I had to come up with an excuse to return home and field my mother's questions. I said I had important work. You don't get it, do you? I remember every detail of that night, Angai. Every single detail. Right from picking you up at the metro station in my car, stopping at the market to buy Sprite for our vodka, to the perfume you wore, and your blue shirt. I remember how we started on the bed and ended up on the floor. We hardly slept that night, no? And the song about the sun you shared the next morning. I remember every-damn-thing!'

Angai opened his mouth to speak, but realized Samar was not done yet.

'You were the only one welcomed into my home,' Samar went on. 'There have been times since then when I have been alone in the house, but I've never had anyone over. I'd be lying if I say I didn't feel the urge to, but I didn't. And I don't think I will ever have the same experience with anyone else. Not even with you, for that matter.'

'That's why we should look forward to newer experiences,' Angai said, stirring his coffee. 'You want some sugar?'

'No, thanks,' Samar replied, taking off his glasses. He stroked his eyebrow with his thumbnail. 'So, this young boy I told you about, I told him as well, about the whole marriage thing, you know. He hates me now. I wonder why. I've never hidden my intentions. I've always been clear about this. I told you too, when we met, that I would eventually get married to a woman, didn't I? He refuses to speak to me because I'm getting married.'

'Well, I can see why,' Angai said.

'What do you mean?'

'Look, you're a perfect model of everything one might want in their partner. You're good-looking, you have a decent career, which means financial security, you're intelligent and you have an amiable personality. Just look at you. You have 'stability' written all over you. So, I understand his disappointment. And on top of that, you're getting married, for crying out loud! I mean, if it was someone else in your place, maybe I would have behaved similarly. You know, Samar, that's the thing with you: you problematize my politics.'

'*Problem-atize!*' Samar said with a frown. 'Don't turn all queer-rights activist on me now.'

'I mean, I have made a stack of all these rules over the years. I write about them, I try so hard to follow them. Some might even say I go on and on about them. Then you waltzed in one fine evening and toppled it all. And I can't help it. Look at us now, so much for my principles: here you are and here I am, sitting with you and sipping coffee,' Angai said. 'I feel like such a hypocrite.'

Neither of them said anything for a few seconds. They looked out of the glass wall from the upper storey of the coffee shop. Their ghostly reflections stared back at them, beyond which, massive buildings gleamed with lights. The year was coming to a close. Soon it would be a thing of the past. If only the past could really be left behind. Angai drew a deep breath and continued, 'You know what, I just want you to be fair to your wife. I don't want her to bear the brunt of … the circumstances.'

'Fair? What do you mean fair?' Samar moaned. Angai shushed him. He then casually glanced around. Thankfully, the place was mostly empty. It was the end of the day, week and even the year. Most offices must be closed. No wonder there were hardly any customers.

Samar repeated the question, this time softly but with renewed intensity: 'What do you mean by fair? Do you mean I should stop talking to you after I'm married? Is that you want?'

Angai knew he didn't want that, and that bothered him.

'And the brunt of what? Of me being myself?' Samar prodded.

'Listen, I know I'm your friend and I should be on your side, even so I can't help but think from her perspective,' Angai said.

'You think from her perspective, she thinks from her perspective, my parents think from their perspective – and no one thinks from mine? My parents aren't willing to wait any longer. They say this is my last chance. I'm trying my best to make this work. I've kept my temper under control countless times and put my ego aside many times already. Even you think I'm being unfair? I won't stop talking to you, okay? I won't stop living *this life*. There are things I'll do for my parents and my wife, but there are some I'll do for *myself* or else I'll lose my self. Isn't that unfair?'

Angai was silent again. A waiter came to their rescue.

'Sir, we are about to close.'

'We are done. Just give us five minutes,' Samar said, without taking his eyes off Angai's face. Angai looked around and realized that the place had emptied out.

'We must start moving. I don't want to miss the last metro,' he said. But before Angai could rise from the couch, Samar scurried past him. Was he more eager to leave? Or had Angai actually let him down?

Samar had stopped at the mouth of the narrow staircase, peering down to see if anybody was coming up. Once sure, he looked at Angai with hopeful eyes. Angai felt a wave of desire awash within him as he inched towards Samar. He leaned against Samar and kissed him.

On his way back in the metro, Angai kept thinking about the episode, replaying each sentence, hoping to find meaning even where there was none. He was reminded of Samar's advice about getting married early. Wasn't he supposed to dig out the Facebook post from the Humans of Delhi page? He had shared it on his wall last week. A few taps on the screen and there emerged a picture of a forty-something woman, dressed in a white kurti and leggings. She stood in a park, bathed in golden sunlight, as if interrupted during her morning walk. A picture of grace. Angai began reading the text below the image.

I am a forty-eight-year-old woman. I came to Delhi with my late husband. Today marks our fourteenth wedding anniversary. I was married for ten years. Kishor was an amazing person and loved me in a way no other man ever could. No other man ever would.

He bought me presents on every anniversary. I must confess, I rarely liked them. He knew it too, yet he never shied away from getting them, which warmed my heart. It was impossible to flaunt them before my friends, or pass them on as heirlooms – not that I have anyone to pass them to – but they were things I always found useful: a cardholder, an ugly yet the most comfortable pair of flip-flops that I still use, a Borosil tiffin set, an egg-beater etc.

Four years ago, on our tenth anniversary, he gave me a present. A present that left me devastated. That morning, he told me he had been diagnosed with advanced stage liver cirrhosis. The offhand manner in which he said it shocked me. But that's how he was. As casual about death as he was about life. Without caring about my reaction, he went on chalking out plans for my future. With his savings and his pension, he added, I would be able to buy a larger house finally.

Once my initial hysteria settled, the extremely loving man he was, he sat me down to explain how this piece of news could be helpful for me. He thought it was a good thing this was how nature had ordained his exit because I would have sought it myself sooner or later. He said he had realized over the years I was not cut out for sharing space, no matter how deeply I loved someone. That's why, he said, I didn't want kids – not because I didn't like them. That's why I found our house tiny – not because it actually was.

The worst part was that I couldn't disagree with him, although I rubbished what he said then. I knew he was right. A part of me felt relieved upon learning he would be gone soon. I absolutely loathe that part of me. My husband was right in saying I would have chosen an exit myself. I didn't have the heart to tell him, as I almost never did, that I was indeed about to ask for a divorce on our anniversary when he told me of his illness, that I loved him for telling me things about me that I myself didn't realize, that I loved him but I couldn't go on living with him. Now that he's actually gone, I miss him terribly.

If you find someone you fall in love with – your soulmate, as it were – please marry them while you are both young or don't marry them at all.

Angai wondered what it must feel like to wake up on the morning of your tenth anniversary, hoping for a divorce, only to learn of your husband's terminal illness. He then imagined Samar as a husband. Would he agree to marry Samar if he had ever proposed? Angai looked out of the window; his station was not far now. He wished the ride could go on longer – not wanting to step out. The train was comfortably warm. No, he would not accept the proposal, he concluded. He didn't love Samar. The yearning and the resentment Samar had evoked in him were partly indulgence and partly addiction, like the outrage he felt against the State's oppressive policies. He may have even felt compelled to cultivate it, had it not organically sprouted from within him. The longing was for a romantic figure who resembled Samar but wasn't really him. Real people were tedious. Angai tried to put himself in the shoes of the woman in the Facebook post. He would sound like her, he thought, as he read through the post again, after ten years of marriage with Samar.

The train came to a sudden halt with the grunt of a prehistoric reptile, making Angai lurch forward.

'*There will be a short delay in this service. We regret the inconvenience*,' announced a dispassionate voice.

Should he finally send a friend request to Samar on Facebook? That way, he could track his downfall year after year. As he was about to type 'Samar' in the search bar, it struck him that Samar's real name was Anirban. On typing the full name, Anirban Bhattacharya, the search results threw up an array of people with the same name. Samar – Angai's Samar – was placed third. The display picture showed a newlywed couple. Samar, wearing a thick garland and an elaborate headgear with two cotton ball-like danglers, stood smiling behind his bride, his arms around hers. The bride's kohl-rimmed eyes were lowered with a coyness as affected as Samar's smile, and her hands filled with what looked like uncooked rice. Angai checked the date. The picture had been uploaded two weeks ago.

He struggled to find a comfortable sitting position as he swiped the screen to view other pictures. His mind first went blank and everything zoomed past in seconds. Disgusted, he put the phone back in his bag. The wait felt endless. He cursed the metro service. But the train stood still stubbornly. He brought out his phone again and typed a long message. He debated which emoji to append. Was he angry? A little. Was he relieved? Absolutely. The train jerked back to life and moved on. He deleted the message.

Tonight too, I sit to unload the squalor of my thoughts onto this paper. Must the paper not resent me?

And while you think that the daily drudgery of life is a battle in itself – a battle to be fought more with yourself than the world outside – life suddenly delivers a blow so staggering that you reel for days, trying to absorb the enormity of it all.

You just look around, amused, as the rest of the world moves on at its usual crazy pace, unmoved by your tragedy. You want the world to explode. You want the people to express profuse regret for what life has done to you. You want the world to come to a halt and tell you how unfair, undeserved and incredible your suffering is. You want all of them to commiserate, yet you feel grated when the platitudes begin to roll out: Keep faith in God. Don't lose hope. Be positive. Stay strong ...

What else can they say? They're not at fault. Perhaps, they're right too. Yet it somehow sounds patronizing. You don't want to answer the calls of the people who ask how you are coping, for that would make you feel helpless all over again; yet you despise those who did not call to check up on you, to extend help. The problem is not them, it's you. It's what the tragedy has made out of you.

You look at yourself in the mirror and realize that you've aged rapidly. You see it on your face, and you feel it in your body. You begin to laugh at people who fuss over petty issues. You begin to hanker after the time you'd fussed over those petty issues. How wonderful those days seem now. You begin to envy everyone around you who leads a normal life and deals with normal problems. You begin to wonder how elusive this one thing has been all your life: normalcy. All your life if there's one thing you've craved immensely, it is: normalcy.

Epilogue

PRANAV BHALLA HAD never waited as eagerly for his friend Namit Kalra as he did today. He had never waited as eagerly for anyone as far as he could remember. They could have met at the funeral of their mutual friend, but Pranav had skipped it. Namit was shocked by Pranav's indifference and had grown resentful of him since. They barely spoke for two years. Pranav had finished a course in filmmaking and had come back to Delhi. He was now a freelance filmmaker. Namit had moved to Bangalore and was struggling to find a co-founder and investors for his tech start-up. When he called up to announce that he was in Delhi for business and wanted to meet, Pranav started thinking of an excuse he could make to avoid the meeting; but Namit said something that forced Pranav to change his mind. He wanted to hand over something to Pranav. 'Rishabh would have wanted you to have it. Please don't be a no-show this time,' Namit had said over the phone. 'Why don't you come over? My parents are away for today,' Pranav had said in reply.

A faint smile gleamed through the cloud of shame on Pranav's face when he saw Namit after two years. His friend had grown bigger. His Facebook pictures couldn't capture any of his clumsiness. The initial awkwardness soon gave way to affection that resurfaced with anecdotes from the past.

'Weren't you looking for an apartment to rent?' Namit asked. 'I saw your post on Facebook.'

'Yeah, I found a place closeby. I'll relocate next week. My parents aren't getting any more liberal with age.' Pranav chuckled. 'What will you eat, tell me?'

'I am not hungry,' Namit said. 'What do you have, though?'

'I'll order something. Chinese?'

After the meal, Pranav gathered the courage to bring up the subject that had been eating him up for days.

'Kalla, how did you get to know?' Pranav said, fidgeting with the remote control.

'About?' asked Namit.

'About Rishabh.'

'Why do you care?' Namit snapped.

When Pranav realized that his silence was not apologetic enough, he said, 'I was in a very dark place then. I had wanted to come but just couldn't. I regret it every day.'

Namit snatched the remote control from his friend and muted the TV. 'I was there when he died, Bhalla,' he said.

'There? As in, Hyderabad-there?'

'There: as in, his-doorstep-there!'

'What are you saying, Kalla?'

'Yes, I'd got to know about the Satyam scam. I was in Bangalore at that time, and Rishabh had stopped answering any calls. You had changed your phone number. Anyway, his father had called me up, all worried, trying to find out about Rishabh. I decided to see him in person and the very next day, I got on a bus. But when I reached your flat and pressed the doorbell, there was no response. The door wasn't locked, so I knew someone was inside. There were several unopened rolls of newspaper lying right by the door. I found that really fishy and went to ask the next-door neighbour.'

'Who? The silver-haired grandmother?'

'Yes, yes, that one. She told me she hadn't seen the fair boy for days now. And the tall one, Rishabh, was also last seen roughly four to five days ago. She thought you guys had gone back home. She mentioned how she dutifully pushed in whatever letters came for him. She didn't bother with the newspapers. I must've looked pretty anxious by then because she asked me if everything was fine. I assured her that it was and went on my way. At that point, I did not know what to do. I even started to think of ways to break into the flat. Then I rang the bell again, longer this time. But no luck. As I turned to get more help, I overheard commotion. Children playing in the compound were howling. And I ran downstairs, without waiting for the elevator ...'

'And ...?' Pranav asked. His throat was dry.

'You know the rest. That idiot jumped right out the window,' Namit said with some difficulty, his voice straining and eyes glistening. 'With the help of others, I managed to rush him to the hospital, but looking at the injuries, I knew there was very little chance.'

'Rascal!' Pranav muttered under his breath.

'How could you have left him alone at a time like that, Bhalla?' Namit asked bitterly.

Pranav couldn't bring himself to say what he wanted to. Instead, he asked, 'Was there any note?'

Namit smirked before he began, 'I went back to the apartment with Rishabh's father. Hearing the commotion, the grandmother next door came out and peeped in. I attended to her and gave Girish uncle some space. She immediately started asking questions. She was fed up with all the uninvited attention and the bad name that place had earned because of Rishabh. 'Nowadays, there is a new variety of rat poison that, after eating, even rats go out of the house to die. Nobody pollutes the place where they live,' she said. She gave me a very dirty look, as if I had pushed Rishabh out of that window. She said she always knew the tall one was up to something, maybe that's why the fair one had left. I somehow managed to make my way inside. I examined the place, trying to imagine the final moments before he jumped. I wonder what must have been going through his mind. The police had found a suicide note already. But it didn't help.'

'What did the note say?'

'Nothing. He blamed no one. No one should be held responsible, he wrote.'

'What was it that you wanted to give to me then?' Pranav asked, as if relieved.

'His journal. I chanced upon it while collecting his books. His father asked me to take them with me. I am sure Rishabh kept it there because he was sure you would take his books. Little did he know you wouldn't even show up at his funeral.'

'Why didn't you tell me all this while? You kept it from me for an entire year?'

'I was furious, you asshole! I couldn't explain your behaviour to myself. Or even his. I felt excluded and betrayed. I used to think we were best friends. Clearly what you guys had was more than friendship. I thought it was unfair that he should die in my arms and yet there be a letter addressed to you. It was unfair that while dying he may have thought of you, and you didn't even turn up at his funeral. I found both of you disgusting.'

Pranav just sat frozen.

Namit grabbed his bag, took out a notebook and flung it at Pranav. 'Here, take this as my last act of kindness, man.'

The notebook landed at Pranav's feet. He stooped to pick it up and held it as though it were some strange object; as though he were unaware of what to do with a notebook, or how to open it.

Namit now put on his shoes and slung his bag on his shoulder, about to leave. He turned back just once to say, 'Dude, if I die will you not come to my funeral either?' Without waiting for a response, he left.

Namit's departure filled the room with a chilling silence. The eerie glow of the light coming from the TV gave the room a haunting ambiance. Pranav opened the notebook and tilted it to catch maximum light. Any other light would have been too strong in this moment. He flipped the pages. Yes, this was Malla's handwriting.

'Tonight, I sit to unload the squalor of my thoughts onto this paper. Must the paper not resent me? Better things could have been written on it ...'

Acknowledgements

THE SEED OF this book came from a quick narrative retelling of a personal experience I had to entertain my Facebook friends.

I had not the faintest idea that I was embarking on a journey that would take the form of a novel and would take nearly a decade to finish. A lot of people have been instrumental in helping me shape the book in its present form and, hence, deserve to be acknowledged and thanked.

My mother, who gave me the gift I cherish the most: a love for words and language.

My friends Pramit Sinha, Ayesha Abrar, Vikram Johari, Kenith Rosario, Tanushree Biswas and Harmeet Kaur, who despite their elevated taste in literature, read my work and encouraged me to write.

Somak Ghoshal, who was the first person who was not on my friend list to have read initial drafts of some of these chapters and said words of praise for the stories that really made me believe this book could go somewhere.

My partner, Shanton Dutta, who not only tolerated my nagging to beta-read the first draft of the chapters – sometimes even on our dates – but also put up with my long absences when I was preoccupied with writing and editing. If this work ever lands up on a list of prescribed texts for some course at a liberal arts university and a hapless student sitting in an exam hall is compelled to comment on or justify the title of the book, they should know they have a bone to pick with Mr Dutta, for he was the one to have suggested it.

Shilpi Bora, my friend, my confidante, who silently cheered for me even when nobody else did.

My supervisors at different times through the writing of this book, Ms Aryama Sakia, Ms Paulami Ghosh and Ms Seema Jerath, who always cut me some slack at work because they realized I was moonlighting as a writer.

Preeti Gill, who showed faith in this book when my own was not very firm. It takes a lot of courage to represent a first-time writer without a pedigree. Thank you, Preeti, for your generosity.

Avneet Kaur, who acquired the book first and made me experience what validation feels like. Isha Banerji, my editor, whose sharp eye helped me weed out clumsy sentences and was tremendously patient with me while I was firefighting on the personal front. (Whatever clumsy prose persists is entirely due to my inability to kill my darlings.) In the same breath, I'd like to thank Shreya Gupta and Shruti Tiwari for ensuring the book comes out error-free.

Devangana Dash, whose unconventional cover design gave an added pop to the book.

The entire editorial team at Pan Macmillan India, who did not throw the manuscript at my face, laughing derisively while I stood before them, pages of the manuscript flying about me – a nightmare that had kept me awake ever since I started sending out the drafts to agents and publishers.